CHASING *the*
Phantom
Ship

CHASING *the* *Phantom Ship*

DEBORAH TOOGOOD

NIMBUS
PUBLISHING

Author's note:
Fox Harbour is a fictional town on the Northumberland
Shore of Nova Scotia.

Nimbus Publishing Limited
3731 Mackintosh St, Halifax, NS, B3K 5A5
(902) 455-4286 nimbus.ca

Printed and bound in Canada

NB1178

Interior design: Jenn Embree
Cover design: Heather Bryan
Cover Illustration: James Bentley, jamesbentley.com

Library and Archives Canada Cataloguing in Publication

Toogood, Deborah, author
Chasing the phantom ship / Deborah Toogood.
Issued in print and electronic formats.
ISBN 978-1-77108-382-9 (paperback).
—ISBN 978-1-77108-383-6 (pdf)
I. Title.

PS8639.O64C53 2016   jC813'.6   C2015-908190-4
                                              C2015-908191-2

Canada

Canada Council   Conseil des arts
for the Arts   du Canada

Nimbus Publishing acknowledges the financial support for its publishing activities from the Government of Canada through the Canada
Book Fund (CBF) and the Canada Council for the Arts, and from the
Province of Nova Scotia. We are pleased to work in partnership with
the Province of Nova Scotia to develop and promote our creative in-
dustries for the benefit of all Nova Scotians.

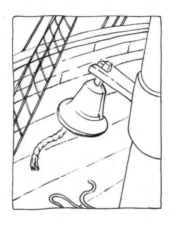

For my parents,
Alma and George Toogood

Chapter 1

❧

My room had a bed that was one metre wide. I know because I measured it for a grade two math project when I was a little kid. There was one dresser, one table from Grandma's, and one wooden chair with a crooked leg that mostly held my clothes so I didn't drop them on the floor. The ceiling sloped down like a triangle and if I wasn't careful, I'd crack my head when I looked out the window. It was a room for one person. Not two.

I stood on my tiptoes to stretch over the dresser. It was already steamy hot and my Barcelona soccer poster curled to the ceiling. I flattened the tape. My cleats lay on top of each other, criss-crossed, in the corner. Mom hadn't made me clean up the red clay stuck on the bottom. She'd rubbed my back, and said even Coach didn't know what a good team player I was. I'd run up and down that muddy field all spring trying to keep up with my best friend Danny.

"Breakfast," Mom called.

I charged down the stairs, my hand gripping the railing while I skipped as many stairs as I dared.

We live in an old farmhouse at the very edge of town. It's not a farm anymore, unless you count the raspberry bushes and the apple trees. And it creaks when the wind blows hard. My parents are do-it-yourselfers, which means we can't afford to pay someone else. It also means I trip over Dad's tools a lot.

My favourite place is my room, because I like to read mysteries. I make up pretend crimes and then write down the clues and put a red check mark by the suspect. I also like being in the kitchen...at least I did. My mom's always in there doing stuff. Our wood stove is there and a big wicker chair with a puffy cushion and Catherine's disgusting play-pen. Not that Mom doesn't clean, it's just that all that baby stuff pushed me out.

"Matt." Catherine giggled and kicked her fat legs against her high chair.

"Honey, watch your sister for a few minutes." Mom wiped the sweat off her face with a quivery yellow glove.

My baby sister annoyed me a lot. If I'd been in charge of choosing my sibling, I would have gone for an older brother; maybe that way I could have had some guidance in the sports department.

"What time does he get here?" I put a piece of toast on Catherine's tray. I waited for her tiny fingers to grab it, and then I snatched it away and buzzed it around her head.

"About four o'clock."

"Four. At least he won't be bugging us for a while."

"Mine." Catherine pushed her mouth down toward the floor and got ready to turn on the waterworks.

"Honestly, Matt, quit teasing your sister.... Another boy in the house will do you good."

The toast came in for a landing. "How come he has to sleep in my room? We don't even know him. He probably snores and talks in his sleep. And he might be really creepy."

"Maybe we should put your cousin in the garage?"

I poured way too much milk onto my cereal, and the circles floated to the top like tiny lifesavers. I put pieces of banana and a handful of blueberries on top. A shipwreck at sea.

"So, have you ever met him?" I asked.

"Twice," Mom said. "Just after he was born, and then again two years ago. He's a good boy, and I expect you to be nice. It hasn't been easy for your Aunt Maddy since her divorce. This visit will be good for the both of them."

The curtains tickled my arm. I pressed my nose against the screen and looked at our sunburned grass in front of the pine trees. But what I couldn't see was the dark blue ocean. I rubbed my arm where the little hairs stood up.

My cousin and I had the same last name. That meant we shared the same DNA, but he grew up in Toronto and that could ruin any relationship. Today he arrived in Fox Harbour.

It was the end of my summer. Adam Simmons was eight years old, and I had to play with him for the next two weeks. Then I'd start grade six. My mom and dad and me have always lived on the Northumberland Shore of Nova Scotia. Right on the edge so I can smell the sea. My only Grampa died two years ago and then Grandma went to live in the home where my other Nanna lives.

"Ah, beautiful day." Dad came into the doorway and stood in his work boots. He reached up and smoothed down his hair. He does that a lot. Making sure it's still there. Everyone says I look like him. That means I'm short—not scrawny short, but a bit thick. And Dad really sucks at sports. Sometimes I wish I had a different dad, but then I feel bad. It isn't his fault he is average, just that it made me average. And Danny is definitely above average.

"Hey," I said as I jumped up from the table.

"What's the rush?" Dad pulled off his boots and sat in his chair.

"Danny and I are building a wharf."

"You'll need Danny to lift those logs," Dad said.

"I wish another storm would dump some logs here."

"How 'bout when I'm in town, I talk to Burt Carter at the lumberyard," Dad said. He put his hands together like a pyramid and pushed his eyebrows together, like he always does when he feels a project coming on.

"Oh lord, don't encourage them," Mom said. "The tide will just drag things out again."

"Boys need a place for their boat." Dad winked at me.

"I wish we could get a new boat, with an outboard motor, like the red one we saw shoot across the harbour on Sunday." My parents gave each other The Look. Work at the plant was slow, and I knew there wasn't a lot of extra money right now. Dad acted extra cheerful, like it didn't matter. Anyway, Danny and I had a plan to fix up my old rowboat. That thing is definitely below average.

"Now, be careful...tide's high," Mom said.

I looked at the clock. Eight thirty. It'd be high tide in an hour. "By three thirty we'll see the sandbars," I said.

"She'll come in quick tonight," Dad said. "Make sure *Ocean Lad*'s pulled up."

"Don't you dare swim without an adult," Mom said.

"Jeez, we're just working on our wharf."

"When Adam gets here he can give you a hand," Dad said.

"I can't wait."

Chapter 2

❦

The screen door snapped shut behind me. I ran around to the front porch, crossed the lawn, and ran through the woods. The trees over my head were so thick it was like being back in my room. The path led me through the prickly bushes and stopped at the top of the cliff. Birds squawked over the seaweed. Waves slapped the rocks. I pulled my ball cap down low and gulped in the salty air.

"Hey, what're you gawking at?" Danny hollered up at me. "Help me with this log."

"Hey yourself." I looked once more at the horizon and climbed down the beat-up steps.

"Come on, we don't have all day."

"Got it." The log fell into my hands and a splinter shoved into my thumb. "Ugh, it's heavy."

Danny was twelve, a year older than me, and stronger than any boy at school. He came first in the Cumberland County wrestling tournament, was MVP of his hockey team, and highest scorer on his soccer team. His room was loaded with hardware.

"Don't drop it," Danny said. His face went all red and he made those big noises like when he lifted his brother's weights.

Danny was shaped like a couch turned on its end. And solid. His whole family was like that. Well, his father and brother. His mother was too, until she got sick and then it got really bad and she died. We went to the funeral at the Anglican church. I'd worried all morning that Danny wouldn't go. He has a phobia about coffins. Like a ghost might float up from the dead. But he sat in the front row wearing a white long-sleeved shirt. That's the only time I've ever seen Danny cry. My mother cried too and Dad was all stiff, then he put his arm on my shoulder.

"Whew, roll it." I dug my toes into the sand and tried to shove the log toward our pile of rocks poking out of the sea. We'd slaved all month stacking those rocks.

"Ready: one, two, three." Danny lifted his end. "Got it, move it more...come on, Simmons."

My arms felt like they were going to pop out of my armpits, but I hung on and we dumped the log onto the rocks.

"Lookit." Wood, in crazy shapes, had been left by the tide.

"Man, what's this?" Danny grabbed a grey plank that curved like a ship's bow.

"It's ancient." I ran my hand over the wood. "Smooth as the beach stones."

"It's from a sunken ship," Danny said. "Jeez, could be haunted." It dropped with a thud on the wet sand. He jumped back. "Let the sea take it...we don't need bad luck."

"Come on, it's just wood."

"No way am I using it. Bet you people died on that. Gramps says these waters are full of pirates."

"Don't you mean 'were'?"

Danny stood there, feet dug into the sand and hands on his hips. He fixed me a good stare. "No, *are*."

My stomach did a little flutter.

"When does your cousin get here?" Danny soaked his size-ten feet in the water.

"Later today."

"You'll be stuck babysitting."

"Hey, I don't plan on losing the rest of my summer. Besides, he might not be that bad." My investigation hadn't given me a lot to go on. Adam had never been to Nova Scotia. He had no brothers or sisters, and his father didn't live with him. He had dark hair like me. I'd helped Mom pick out Lego for him last Christmas. On his first day of school he had run from his desk up the street to the cemetery, where he threw himself down by the largest gravestone. Aunt Maddy had made him promise not to run from school again. And he kept it.

"What time is it?"

"Eleven thirty-one." Danny had the coolest watch. It could go one hundred feet under water.

"Whoa! My boat." *Ocean Lad* bobbed free at the edge of the water.

"Grab her, Simmons. Jeez, tie better knots."

"Okay, I got her..."

"I'm just telling you, don't want to be losing your boat." Danny shoved her up to the dry sand.

I wound the rope around the large rock three times and tied my special reef knot. "Tide's never come this high." I stood over our fire pit. Seawater dripped off burnt pieces of wood. Other than that, everything looked normal. That should be the first clue for a detective.

I plunked down on the log behind the fire pit.

"Oh man, did you hear? We have a chance at the finals." Danny kicked at an invisible ball. "Can't wait to cream those guys from Amherst."

I concentrated on digging a hole in the sand with my heel.

"Hey, we've got one of the best teams. Stewart's gone next year...get some muscle, there might be a spot."

Who was he kidding? They were above average. Unless half the team dropped dead, my chances were nil.

"Emma's team beat Oxford four to one last night," he said.

Emma Miller had been in my grade since primary. She and Danny were my only neighbours, if you just counted the kids. That made them my best friends by geography. Emma played soccer and basketball, but she took everyone in sailing. Another above-average kid.

"Did you get the hot dogs?" I asked. "And Mitch?"

"Yeah, he said he'd come."

My mom tends to freak out if I light a fire. Danny's brother Mitch just turned sixteen, so that made it okay. I picked up my roasting stick and rubbed the whittled end.

"Adam might like this." Part of me was excited to have my cousin visit, but I worried Danny might not think it was so great having a little kid around.

We lay back on the hard-packed sand. The small waves rolled up, reached for our feet, then pulled back to the sea.

༄

"Man, it's hot," I said, wiping sweat from my upper lip. We were walking along the beach, kicking at the water.

"Tide'll be all the way out by four," Danny said.

Twice a day the tide pulled the ocean back. Then we could run on the sandbars. We mostly threw sand at each other and goofed around. Our beach never got crowded.

"I saw you boys working hard." Mrs. Miller stood in water up to her knees. Like a lifeguard, she held one hand over her eyes and watched the sea. I had never seen her wear a bathing suit, and didn't want to think about her saving anyone.

DEBORAH TOOGOOD

"Can you watch us?" I asked.

"Sure, Emma's over there under the umbrella writing up a storm."

"Hey Emma, good game last night," Danny said.

"Thanks." She ducked her head down. She had on a red, too-big T-shirt and her mother's sunglasses, which made her look like a ladybug. Besides being neighbours, Emma and I had reading in common. The same stories made us laugh and she liked a good adventure. But this summer she'd been hanging out more with the girls from town.

"Yeah, good game," I added. "What are you reading?"

"Nothing, just writing some things down." She closed her book.

"Coming for a swim?" Danny asked her.

"Maybe later, I want to finish this before Mom and I go to Amherst."

With that, she went back to it. I wondered what she was writing about.

Chapter 3

❧

I ate two tuna melts for lunch and one cookie, then helped Dad rake the grass. I dumped the last pile at the back of our land. Just as I turned to go, something sparkled in the sunlight. An old coin. Correction: an ancient coin. I pried it out of the ground. It was copper-coloured like a penny, but the green age spots made it difficult to see the etching on the metal. I couldn't make out the first two numbers, but the last two were "68."

"What are you up to this afternoon?" Dad asked.

"Nothing much." This was usually enough information for parents and it allowed me to get away. Besides, I wanted to enjoy my last few hours alone. Two weeks until school, and so far summer had been kind of boring with Danny and Emma playing so much soccer.

I lay on my bed and fingered the coin. Two ancient things in one day. I'd list them in my notebook. A superstitious person would look for three, but I was thinking like an investigator.

I watched a fly buzz between the screen and the window. Its wings beat wildly. "Just go, the window is open." Stupid fly. The rusty screen gave me some trouble and I had to give it a big jerk. And then it fell down on the lawn. The fly made its escape just as a car parked in our driveway. I sped down the stairs, across the blue linoleum Mom wanted to tear up, and stopped in the doorway. Mom and Dad hugged Aunt Maddy. Dad gave Adam one of his friendly punches to the shoulder, then shook his hand. Adam stood half behind his mother. He wore long pants and blinding white sneakers.

"Matt, for heaven's sake, come here." Mom waved me out of the doorway.

"You're so big!" Aunt Maddy wrapped both arms around me and gave me a hard squeeze. My nose squished into the scratchy material of her shirt. She smelled like French fries. I pushed back. "Adam, this is your cousin Matt."

"Hi." He was missing his two front teeth. The only word that came to my mind was *petite*. Seriously. The Simmons clan might be short, but we're not petite. And I sensed a nerd.

"Hi," I said.

We stared at each other, Adam's arms straight down like a soldier. I put my hands in my pockets, turned, and shuffled after the adults.

"Kate, are you still winning ribbons at the county fair?" They stood among my mother's skyscraper gladiolus.

"Every September," Dad said, putting his arm around Mom.

"It's the secret ingredient," I said.

"What?" Adam asked.

"Manure," I said.

Adam scrunched up his nose and stepped back onto the walk.

"We have to get a picture," Aunt Maddy said. "Adam, get the camera."

Mom picked up Catherine and stood close to Dad. I stood in front.

"Me, too." Adam pushed in beside me.

"Say cheese!" Aunt Maddy snapped the picture with the fanciest camera I'd ever seen.

I stared at the photo Aunt Maddy had taken. Adam's shoulder was touching my elbow. He looked like my little brother.

Chapter 4

The green air mattress sat in the box. I smoothed out the creases and stuck in the pump. Air filled the first column.

"Can I do it?" Adam jumped off my bed.

"Just press with your foot," I said. Our house had never had a guest room until last week. I had helped move the single bed from Catherine's room downstairs to Mom's sewing room, which used to be Grandma's room. Catherine didn't need it yet, and Aunt Maddy said it was just perfect.

"It's ready." Adam pushed the plump mattress against my bed.

"You'll have more space over here." I put it next to the desk. That gave me half a metre.

Adam rolled onto his bed, pulled a crumpled Kleenex out of his pocket, and wiped his nose. He didn't sit still for long.

"Is that yours?" His hand touched my only award, Most Improved Sailor.

"Yeah." Last summer my father signed me up for sailing camp. For two weeks I tried to sail a laser in a circle in the harbour. Two kids sat in each boat taking turns pushing the till and ducking when the boom came around. Jumping off the wharf at the end of the day was way more fun. However, with Emma's coaching, I'd made some progress.

"Is it gold?" His hand rubbed the single sail.

"Maybe."

"I have a ribbon from the school science fair," Adam said.

"Is that so?" I said.

"Whose dog?" Adam grabbed Sandy's picture. She lay on the sand, in the shadow of *Ocean Lad*. She was nine years old in people years.

"Don't touch that."

"Sorry." Adam's lips went down like Catherine's.

"She's gone." Sandy died a year and a half ago, two days after Christmas. She'd thrown up all night. I had to take her out into the snowbank, but it was too cold. Then we just gave up on keeping the floor clean and sat with her in a corner of the kitchen. The next morning she lay quiet on my lap while Dad drove us to Dr. Willowby's. When the doctor pushed the needle into her leg, her head stayed still, and her golden tail didn't thump the steel table.

"What happened?"

"She ate a box of chocolates, the whole thing, even the box."

Adam stared at the photo.

"Is that your boat?" His finger hovered over the picture, careful not to touch.

"Yeah, it's called *Ocean Lad*, that was Sandy's official name."

"I'm getting a dog," Adam said.

"What kind?"

"A big one." Adam stretched his hands out wide. "The kind that saves people. Are you getting another one?"

"Someday. Last spring the lady at the post office had puppies for sale, but they weren't the right kind."

I had gone to look. Three brown puppies lay squished together in a cardboard box. The post office lady placed each one on the floor. I picked up the brave one, placed my hand on his head, and slid it down to his skinny tail. His fur wouldn't lie down the right way. I thanked the lady and put the puppy back in his box.

"Want to see the beach?" I asked, wedging his suitcase into the corner.

"Are we allowed?"

"Yeah. First rule, no long pants."

Adam unzipped his knapsack. "Mr. Teddy." He squeezed the glass-eyed bear.

"He can sit on your bed, we won't be long," I said.

"I'm sure everything—" Dad stopped talking as we came down the stairs. Mom frowned at the teapot, and Aunt Maddy twisted a tissue between her hands. The three of them were sitting around the kitchen table, a plate of untouched cookies sitting in front of them.

"Hey there, where you boys off to?" Dad asked.

"I want to show Adam the beach."

"Matt, it's almost dinnertime," Mom said.

"Danny and I were planning a bonfire, I told you yesterday...we're roasting hot dogs."

"Well—" Mom wiped sweat from her face. "Adam just got here, do you have to run off and see Danny?"

"You said." I reached for two cookies.

"Can we? Please?" Adam asked.

For once Catherine's timing was good, and this time she really cranked it up. Her cry bounced off the kitchen walls all the way from her bedroom.

"I'll get her." Aunt Maddy jumped up, dropping tissues on the floor.

"Please? I promised Danny, and Mitch will be there."

"We can probably find some marshmallows around here," Dad said.

"I know where they are." I ran into the pantry, a skinny closet, the shelves full of jars of pickles and jam. A bowl of fat strawberries sat on the shelf. I stuffed one into my mouth and grabbed a bag of marshmallows.

"Let's go," I said to Adam.

"There'll be some dinner left over, just in case," Mom called out after us.

Chapter 5

❧

Adam followed so close behind me that his foot yanked off the back of my sneaker.

"Hey." I stopped to push my heel back in.

"Did you know my father doesn't live with us anymore?" Adam asked.

"Yeah..."

"We moved. To an apartment. We're really high, on the twelfth floor."

"How are you going to have a dog there?"

"I can if I want."

I walked faster and faster until we stood at the top of the cliff.

"Woah...the ocean." Adam stopped and stared.

Down below I could see Danny sitting on our bit of wharf, skipping stones.

"That's my friend Danny. Don't say anything stupid, okay? Now, follow me. And hang onto the railing."

"Ow!" Adam stuck his thumb in his mouth.

"Be careful, the wood is picky."

Adam turned his back to the beach and climbed down the steep stairs as if he was on a ladder.

"What did you expect? An elevator?" I went ahead and jumped over the last few stairs into the sand. Adam picked his way down to the bottom. I waved at Danny and pointed to Adam. Danny shrugged.

"Wow, it's so big!" Adam ran to the water's edge and threw his arms out wide.

I stood on the sand between Danny and Adam. I wanted to show Adam the tiny crabs in the hard-packed sand, and the little holes that squirted clam juice on my legs when I stepped on them, and the jellyfish to scoop and the seaweed to pop, but Danny was waiting for us.

"Hey Adam, come over here." I waved at him to join us. "Well, he's here," I said. Next to Danny, Adam looked pink and skinny. The branches on the willow tree in our yard were thicker than his arms.

"Hey." Danny rolled his eyes at me. "You're six?"

"I'm eight." Adam said. He moved closer to me, and for a second I was worried he was going to hold my hand. I jumped away.

"Holy cow, the tide is way out," I said. "I can see the third sandbar." Our beach looked like a desert, and the water lay between the sandbars like small ponds.

"It's starting to come in," Danny said. "It's almost six o'clock."

"Mostly we have two sandbars," I told Adam. "Tide's extra low today. I've never explored the third one."

Adam ran to the water and stopped at the edge. Then he jumped up and down like he was possessed. "This is fun," he said. "You're lucky."

He ran around like a small pup, then stopped and pointed to our wharf. "What's that?"

"It's a wharf for my boat. When the tide gets in I can tie *Ocean Lad* to it.

"You've never seen a wharf?" Danny said.

"Not like yours."

I looked at our pile of rocks and wood. "We built it ourselves."

Danny picked up his bag and took some matches out.

"Isn't Mitch coming?" I asked.

"No." Danny threw down the grocery bag. "Dad found some cigarettes in Mitch's room. He's grounded."

Danny didn't say much about home. He didn't hang around there a lot. Sometimes Mom asked him to supper, and she always sent him home with a jar of something.

"We can have a fire tomorrow," I said.

"Don't be a baby," Danny said. He picked up some dry seaweed and pushed it under the tangled wood. Adam crouched down to watch him light the match.

"Darn." Danny lit three more matches. The seaweed crackled, and a puff of smoke twisted up in a thin column. "Blow."

Our knees sank into the sand and our noses touched the charred wood. Adam and I blew at the seaweed. The thin curl of smoke vanished.

"It's too damp," I said, fanning the wood with my hands.

Danny kicked sand on the fire pit. "You smothered it."

"Maybe we can find some drier wood," I said.

Adam picked up some twigs.

"Never mind." Danny took a hot dog from the package and bit off a piece. "Here." He held out the half-eaten hot dog to Adam.

"No thanks." Adam dropped the sticks.

"Come on, it won't hurt you." Danny stuck out the package, but Adam didn't budge.

"Hey, what about me?" I took one of the raw hot dogs, bit off a small piece, and swallowed it. It was kind of like that gross canned meat.

Danny and I sat down near the fire pit. He tore open the plastic bag of buns and three fell in the sand. Adam hesitated, then reached down and, one by one, picked them up. He tried to shake the sand off.

"Afraid of a little dirt?" Danny asked.

Adam looked at me, his lip drooping again.

"Come on, he's just trying to help," I said. Boy, was Danny in a mood. "Here." I put some ketchup on Adam's bun and then spread some on my own cold dinner.

Adam poked a jellyfish with a seashell. "What's this?" The red glob quivered.

"Don't you know where jelly comes from?" Danny asked.

"It's a fish," I said.

Long, hairy strings stretched out on the sand behind the round blob.

"How will it get to the water?"

"Don't worry, the tide will rescue it," I said.

"Or drag it to its death," said Danny.

Chapter 6

❦

"Let's go out there." Danny pointed to the third sandbar.

I kicked at the water. "I have to stay with Adam."

"Come on, before the tide comes in. It's not deep." Danny threw his T-shirt on the sand and did a bellyflop in the shallow water.

"I don't know...." The water didn't even reach the bottom of Danny's shorts. "We could wade a bit."

"I'm really hot." Adam pulled his shirt off and threw it on the sand like Danny.

"Look." Danny laughed at the tan line that stopped at Adam's elbows.

I shook my head and dropped my shirt. "Let's go." A few metres away, ripples of water broke on the dry sand. The tide had turned.

Danny practiced handstands beside me while I sat on the first sandbar waiting. Adam stood ankle-deep in water.

"Yikes—fish!" He tore back to the safety of the beach.

"It's just minnows. Splash the water and they'll take off," I shouted.

"Come on," Danny said. "It's not deep—we don't have all night."

"Yeah." I waved him out. "You're safe with us, we're just wading."

Adam waded back into the water and picked his way to the first sandbar.

"It's going to be a slow two weeks," I said to Danny.

The three of us started wading to the second sandbar, the water so low it barely touched my belly button.

"Let's see who can do the dead man's float the longest," Danny said.

Adam surprised me by throwing himself, belly first, into the water. I lay face down, my body shaped like a cross, the water holding me up and tickling my ears. I pretended to sleep, until I burst to the surface and gulped for air.

"Ugh, it tastes awful." Adam spat out the water.

I liked the saltiness of the ocean. After a swim, I'd lie on my towel and lick the salt off my arm.

"I win!" Danny threw his arms up into the air.

We sat on the second sandbar.

"What's that land over there?" Adam pointed across the Northumberland Strait.

"That's PEI," I said. "Prince Edward Island."

"Can we take a boat there?" Adam looked toward shore at my rickety rowboat.

"You can't row against the current out there. Besides, that old thing would be sitting on the bottom before you reached the point," I said.

"Let's go," Danny said, pointing at the third sandbar.

I looked at it. A giant rock stuck up in the middle. My heart raced. I wanted to explore it.

"It's too deep." I looked at Adam. "You wait here."

"Are you coming or not?" Danny asked.

DEBORAH TOOGOOD

"I don't want to stay here," Adam said.

"Come on." Danny fell backward into the water and began to swing his arms like a windmill.

"Can you swim?" I asked Adam.

"Of course, I'm not a baby." Chest first, he dropped into the water and thrashed about like Mrs. Jeckel's old retriever. He could stay afloat.

"Wait up!" I shouted after Danny.

I pulled out my best crawl stroke but couldn't catch him. I let my feet drift down to the cold water near the sandy bottom. I could see Danny almost at the sandbar and heard Adam splashing behind me. Finally, my feet sank into sand and I crawled onto the sandbar. I turned to watch Adam.

"It's not much farther," I shouted. His nose bobbed just above the water, and his hands were moving too fast. He was in panic mode, but he was making progress.

"Almost there! You can do it," I said. "Come on." Adam dragged himself out on shaky legs and lay on the wet sand. His small chest heaved up and down. He spat out salt water.

"Over here!" Danny waved at me.

I had never seen this rock up close. Once, Dad and I had tried to bring the boat in, but we hadn't wanted to get swamped. Like a mountain, the granite rock went straight up. Taller than me.

"Man, it's so cool." I walked around the perimeter.

"What's this?" Danny scraped at the barnacles clinging to the rock.

I tore at the slimy seaweed. "Look." Faint markings trailed across one side of the rock, like the engravings on the old tombstones in the graveyard. My detective senses started to tingle. "It's a cross and some numbers."

Danny stared at the chiselled figures. "It says '1868'... it's a marker. I bet they put a dead man here."

"Who did?" Adam asked.

"Pirates," Danny said. "Gramps said their ghosts haunt the water."

I put my nose right up to the markings. They'd been here a long time, that's for sure.

"I don't like ghosts," Adam said.

"Those are just stories." The wind lifted the hair on my arms and I shivered.

"I'm not so sure," Danny said.

Adam didn't look convinced. I leaned over and whispered in his ear. "Danny just likes to exaggerate. Want to build a sandcastle? The wet sand packs really well."

"You help too." Adam turned and ran to the middle of the sandbar, then bent down and started digging in the sand.

"What's that?" Danny plunked down beside Adam.

"I'm building a sandcastle."

"You need more sand if you want a real castle." Danny began to scoop fistfuls of sand into a pile.

The three of us crouched down on our knees, our bare backs to the sky; we worked and worked to make a mountain of sand. Adam scooped out a round moat and piled the wet sand in the middle. We made turrets and walls and decorated them with mussel shells. The heat of the sun disappeared. I crouched so long the sand ground into my knees. The moat slowly filled with water. We didn't notice the sandbar growing smaller.

Chapter 7

❦

Grains of sand shifted under my feet, water covered the sandbar, and the wind tugged at my shorts.

"Hey, we have to head in," I said.

"The waves are crashing over our moat." Adam packed sand onto the battered walls.

"We're under attack!" Danny kicked at the rising water.

I looked toward shore. Water was creeping over the second sandbar. While we'd been working on our castle, the tide had come in. How could I have let so much time pass? I knew better. The wind didn't help; it whipped the waves up and swimming would be tough. We'd have to battle the current.

"Come on, guys, we have to go!" I said.

Danny led. We each took five steps, then the ocean floor fell away. Adam disappeared. He came up spitting water and thrashing out the dog paddle. I tried to follow Danny. Salt spray blew in my face and waves slapped against my chest. I treaded water. The beach looked farther away than it had in the afternoon.

Adam crawled back to the third sandbar, the waves breaking at his knees. I followed him. Danny swam almost halfway back to the second sandbar. I could see how hard he was working to keep his head above the waves. The tide tore down the walls of our castle. The water was now much deeper between the sandbars.

"How will we g-get back?" Adam asked. His lower lip quivered.

"Danny!" I yelled and pointed to the large rock.

"I could swim to shore...get a boat." A wave clobbered him. He came up spitting salt water.

"We should stay together." I glanced at Adam.

"We'll be stuck here—"

"It's too far now, and there are whitecaps." I shouted over the wind.

Another wave hit Danny. He struggled to his feet and lurched back to safety. "Your stupid cousin."

It wasn't just Adam; I had serious doubts about swimming that distance in rough water. "We'll be safe here." I was sure someone would see us before the tide covered the rock. I put my foot in a crack and pulled myself up the side of the rock. "Ow." My knee scrapped over the rough stone and blood ran onto the carvings in the ocean tombstone.

"Make some room." Danny heaved himself up. "Adam, grab my arms." Adam stuck out his hands and let Danny pull him up.

The water swirled below, like a bathtub slowly filling. I stared across the water at the empty shore. I would get it when I got home.

"Your dad will be looking for us," I said.

"I told him I was eating with you."

"My parents think we're with Mitch." I could see them sitting around the kitchen table. The plates would be scraped and piled in the sink and Dad would be starting on his second slice of apple pie. And there would be tea. "This is just great. We're stuck here and no one knows."

"I'm cold." Adam hugged his legs to his chest.

"These rocks are high...it won't be long. Someone is always walking on the beach." I squeezed closer to Adam.

No one talked. The waves bashed against the rock with a steady rhythm, the water creeping up. I stared at the shore, willing my father to come looking for us.

"I can make it," Danny said.

I shook my head. "It's too dangerous."

"My old man will kill me if he catches me out here."

"We have to wait." Panic filled me. I'd let Adam come out here. Daylight was fading.

"This is nuts. It's almost nine o'clock," Danny said. "At high tide, these rocks will be covered."

"I want to go home." Tears started down Adam's cheeks.

"Someone will see us—"

"No, they haven't, I should've kept going...it's a tough swim now." Danny stood up, stuck his arms straight out, and jumped off the rock.

"Danny!"

He vanished under water before bursting to the surface. For a moment the water gripped him against the rock, but suddenly he shoved off, his legs thrusting him forward. Then one large wave slammed into the back of his head. He disappeared.

Chapter 8

❦

"**D**anny!" I stared at the ocean, sure that at any minute his head would pop up and he'd laugh at me. Adam, silent, curled into a ball and rocked back and forth.

"There he—no. Must have been a fish." I watched as the dark waves rolled by.

"Matt." Adam's voice cracked and his shoulders shook.

I stared at the sea. *Please, please be okay.* Bubbles trailed across the water; they could have been from Danny or just from the waves. The wind pulled and screamed in my ears. *Oh lord, someone help us, please, Danny has to make it.* I pushed the panic back down my throat. *Keep calm, it's a bad dream, it'll be all right.*

"Don't worry, Danny's tough. A wave won't keep him down...he'll make it."

"How long will it take him to get help?" Adam had his arms wrapped around his legs. He looked about the size of a basketball.

"Soon." My heart thumped. Why did Danny have to do something crazy? This was suicide. Adam was my responsibility.

"I see him!" Adam pointed at the black water.

I crouched down. "It's nothing." My breath pushed out.

"I don't like it here." Adam clenched my arm.

We sat on the rock, our bodies wedged together. *Think,* I told myself, but my thoughts paralyzed me. *Danny swam to shore because he didn't think I could make it.* I needed to do something.

"If we shout really loud, someone might hear us," I said, and began yelling. "Help! Help!"

Adam let out a scream bigger than he was. "Help! Please help!"

"Save us! Help!" I screamed.

The wind blew offshore and our voices went out to sea. We were screaming to no one. I strained to see the beach. Danny might be there by now; his father had a motorboat, and with a light, they could find us. I put my arm around Adam's shoulders and crouched on the bit of rock sticking out of the water. The ocean had risen about a metre, covering the sandbars and washing the crabs back to the sea. The tide would carry away our shirts and shoes, removing any clue as to where we were.

I prayed Danny would make it.

Chapter 9

❦

I saw it move. Something in the dark was floating toward us. "Look." I pointed at the shadow bobbing on the waves.

"It's…a log," Adam said.

"I can grab it." The driftwood dipped into the hollow of the wave.

"There—"

"Ugh, I can't." I willed my arms longer.

"T-try again," Adam said.

A wave floated the log closer to our rock.

"Hold onto me." I stretched out on my belly and Adam grabbed my ankles. Waves sloshed in my face. Adam's hands slipped down to my heels and then salt water filled my mouth. I somersaulted into the sea. The cold shocked me. My eyes burned, but I wouldn't take them off the dark spot above me. Pushing up, I threw both arms over the driftwood, too stunned to care when it smashed against the rock. The salt water stung where the skin had scraped off my knee. I held on.

"Adam, grab it," I gasped. Another wave swept over me. He didn't move.

"I can't hold it myself."

Adam reached out one hand, unwilling to move from his spot on the rock.

Whack! The driftwood smashed into the rock. My grip loosened.

"Help me!" A monster wave crashed over my head. I lost my hold, and floated in the quiet water under the surface before I burst up, sucking in as much air as I could. I kicked hard. Our rock looked like an iceberg, a tiny bit of it protruding above the water. Desperate kicks pushed me back to Adam. *Breathe.* Like a seal I beached myself on the rock; it was no longer necessary to climb up. Adam came to life and helped me slide back to safety. I began to shake as if it were winter.

"I'm sorry." Adam began to cry.

"It was a stupid idea. We can't float on a piece of driftwood," I said between gulps of air.

"It wasn't stupid."

I looked at Adam. Soon we would have to make a move.

"When are they coming to rescue us?"

"They're getting the boat ready now." I figured we had thirty minutes left on the rock. Once we entered the water, they'd never find us.

When the sun disappeared, so did the wind. But I was worried about the current. I had never tried to swim that far, and the black water terrified me. How would I hang onto Adam?

The water beat against the rock like the ticking of a clock.

Adam half-sat on me. "What are we—"

"Something's out there." I strained to see. "Listen." I could hear the slapping of water against wood.

"There!" Adam pointed. "It's a boat."

The clouds covering the moon shifted enough for me to see a small boat about twenty metres away.

"Over here!" Adam screamed. "Help!"

"It's sitting too high, it's got to be empty."

There was no time to think about the consequences. I slid off what was left of our rock and did my best to swim toward the boat. The crawl-stroke propelled me forward. The boat dipped in front of me. Grabbing the side, I hung there for a second. I took a deep breath and with all my might heaved myself over the gunnel. My heart lifted when I fell against the boards and I dared to breathe again. But I had no time. A wave pushed the boat toward the rock. I grasped the familiar rope tied to the bow and flung it at Adam.

"Hang on," I shouted. I wasn't even close. *Calm down.* I yanked it back and threw the rope again. "Grab it."

He did.

"Now slide into the water, I'll pull you." He didn't even have to move; small waves were washing over the rock as I pulled him toward the boat.

Adam kept his head up and his mouth sealed, his small legs kicking up a storm. I kept working the rope into the boat. His legs were still dangling overboard when a wave broadsided us and tilted the boat. We sat down hard in the water sloshing in the boat's bottom.

"It's *Ocean Lad*, my boat." My hands unclenched, and the tightness in my stomach let go.

"How do we make it go?" Adam clung to the old rope.

"The oars are at the house." I grinned at Adam. "But we have a boat."

"Yeah, good riddance to the rock."

Ocean Lad drifted in the dark. The current was moving away from shore, and us along with it. The lights from the houses blurred and seem to shrink as I stared at them.

DEBORAH TOOGOOD

Adam sniffled. I crawled over to him. "See the moon? It makes the tide rise and fall. Sometimes it changes position and we have extreme tides, like today."

"Every day?"

"Every twelve hours, high tide pushes onto the beach." I settled beside Adam, my back against the bow.

"Where is everyone?" Adam's shivered in his soggy clothes.

"Don't worry, they'll find us." I liked having his shoulder against mine, even if it was his fault I was stuck out here.

The bottom of my wooden rowboat was worn from dragging it over the rocks, and the patches Dad and I put on last summer had started to lift. I never took it out anymore.

"It's a good thing Danny swam to shore, we'd be like sardines in here," Adam said.

Ocean Lad was almost a metre wide and about a metre and a half long. A plank made up the seat across the middle and another one ran against the stern. I'd stripped my boat bare except for the nylon rope tied to an old soup can and the rope tied to the bow. The can had been necessary ever since *Ocean Lad* sprung a leak last summer.

"It's better than the rock." The can floated in the two centimetres of water in the bottom of the boat.

"Do you think he's okay?"

"Sure, Danny's strong." It felt like midnight. He must have had time to get to shore and come back. Where was he?

"We're safe now, aren't we?"

"The fishing boats will be out at dawn...they'll see us." Even if Danny got back to the rock, he'd never spot us. Fog was hugging the water. The lights on shore had disappeared.

The water in the bottom rolled from bow to stern. I should've started bailing, but my arms didn't want to move. Exhaustion pulled at me. I would rest a few minutes and then get to work with the soup can.

Cold water trickled in my ears.

"Wake up!" I shouted.

It was pitch black and our boat felt like a bathtub. My heart pounded in my throat.

"Start bailing." I grabbed the can and scooped water. Adam bailed with his hands. We bailed and bailed. It wasn't enough. The old boat was taking on water faster than we could get it out.

"I can't, it keeps coming in." Adam's arms dropped.

"Keep working," I yelled.

She would stay afloat two more hours, maybe.

Chapter 10

❦

"**D**on't drink that." I took the can away from Adam.
He blinked back tears. "I'm thirsty."

"That'll make it worse." My tongue stuck to my mouth.
"One night without water won't kill us. Come on, we have
to keep bailing." Like a robot, I scooped the water and threw
it overboard. Adam lay slumped in the bow; every few minutes, he cupped his leaky hands to toss out the water. I didn't
blame him. His first trip here had turned into a nightmare.

I gazed at the blackness. The sun was long gone and
goosebumps covered my arms. No shadows to show the out-
line of land and not a flicker of light. I hadn't a clue where
we were.

"Take a break if you have to," I said.

"It's okay." Adam sat up.

We worked steadily, and the level of water in the boat
stayed the same. Maybe *Ocean Lad* would make it. Adam
slowed, then stopped. Water slapped the hull.

"Hey." He pointed toward the stern. "Look...what's...
what's that?"

A red glow shaped like a half moon grew in the sky.
Fog swirled around it and blurred the lines like a smoke-
screen. We drifted closer. Three columns rose up through
the flickering sky.

I was staring at a fire on water.

"Maybe it's flares," Adam said. "They've come to rescue us!" He waved his arms wildly in the air.

For one minute, hope formed in my gut. Could it be the coast guard? Clouds shifted in front of the moon and I strained to see. A creepy feeling climbed my spine.

"Those aren't flares."

Our tiny boat pushed closer to what looked like a three-masted schooner, swallowed by fog and leaping flames. But it was quiet. Too quiet.

We were about fifty metres away when the red glow faded and disappeared into the fog. We sat in the dark.

"Pirates," Adam whispered.

"It can't be."

"Danny said so."

"More like a hallucination," I said. "Sometimes people see things—"

"We both saw it. It was a big boat on fire!" Adam's voice rose to a loud pitch.

"Whatever it was, it's gone now."

I looked at the water still collecting in the bottom of our boat. I had no idea what time it was, but at dawn the fishing boats would be out. We had to hold on.

Adam sniffled. On my knees, I squeezed my eyes shut and prayed. *Dear God, I know I didn't weed Mom's garden like I was supposed to, and I went swimming when I shouldn't, and I'm especially sorry I brought Adam out here...I know this is bad, but we don't deserve to drown. If you could please hurry morning,*

I promise to be good. I thought of throwing in a few Hail Marys, like I'd seen Willy McInnes do, but I wasn't Catholic and this wasn't the time to offend God.

I opened my eyes. In the blackness I saw a tiny light. A star. It faded away. I shook my head and waited. There. It hung low to the water. A small light?

"Someone's coming," my voice cracked. "Hey," I called.

"I see it." Adam jumped up.

We waved our arms wildly. "Help!"

Out of the fog appeared an old dory. The oars dipped in and out of the water as the boat worked steadily toward us. We waited. Up and down the waves carried the boat. Getting closer and closer.

"Someone's come to get us!" Adam shouted. "We're here!"

An old man. Grey hair hanging down to his shoulders. His ragged clothes flapped in the wind. He looked like a skeleton.

"Help!" I leaned over the side as far as I dared. "Save us!" Silence.

"Hey! Over here!" The fog must be muffling my voice.

He didn't turn his head or shift his body, but the boat slowed. Salt ringed his eyes and formed a white crust on his bushy eyebrows. His skin was leather.

"He's going to hit us," Adam whispered.

More than that, this guy was totally creepy. My heart hammered in my chest. Water covered my feet.

"Grab the side when he gets close."

Adam crouched down in the stern, his fingers dug into the seat.

The old wood dory pulled alongside. The man stayed bent over his oars. Waiting.

"Adam, help me, grab the side."

"No...he looks like a...g-ghost."

The man's clothes were ragged, almost transparent, and the fog blew all around us.

"You're getting in." I pulled at Adam's arm. "This boat's sinking."

"No."

"I'll go first." I took a deep breath and stuck one bare foot over the side. It brushed the rough boards. "Adam, move it." I held the gunnel. *Ocean Lad* listed badly to port, water trickled over the side, and then, like a dam breaking, the water roared in.

Adam had one foot over the side, straddling the two boats. *Ocean Lad* shifted and smashed my knuckles.

"Ow!"

"Hurry," Adam cried, teetering.

"Hang on!" I screamed. A wave dumped more water into *Ocean Lad*, I yanked Adam's arm, and we tumbled into the bottom of the mysterious dory.

The old man held the boat steady.

"She's going down!" I cried. Inch by inch, *Ocean Lad* disappeared into the sea. I had no time to mourn her loss, and told myself that she had had a burial at sea like that of the greatest ships.

The old man began to row. Adam crawled to the front and sat on the small wooden seat. My two shipmates said nothing. The blood pounded in my ears. Adam and I huddled in the bow, sitting as far away from the salty sailor as we could. The shadow from the oil lamp distorted his face. A red scar twisted across his cheek, and a black gap appeared where there should be a tooth.

I shifted my weight and cleared my throat. It was spooky, but I was sitting in a boat that wasn't sinking. Near my feet, the moonlight struck something small and shiny; I leaned down to get a better look, thinking it might be a clue as to who this strange man was. I would check it out when we got home and return it later. I slipped it into my pocket.

"We're sure glad to see you," I said.

Silence.

Maybe he didn't hear me.

"Where are you from?"

The only answer was the steady dipping of oars.

Chapter 11

❧ ❧

I jerked awake. The boat thumped bottom, rocked a bit, then stopped. Land. I didn't care where. We were safe.

"Adam, wake up, wake up, we're on shore!"

"What?" Adam rubbed his eyes.

I jumped over the bow and landed in ankle-deep water. "Grab my hand." I dragged Adam over the side of the boat and out of the water. "Come on." My toes dug into land.

"We made it!" I jumped in the sand. "Hey." I turned to thank our rescuer. "Where did he go?" I looked back. The fog lay like a blanket over the water. It blocked any chance of the moonlight showing us where he went. "He's gone."

"That's because he's a ghost."

"Oh, come on. There's got to be an explanation."

"He was scary," Adam said.

"But he saved us." I shivered.

I checked the pockets of my waterlogged shorts and pulled out the piece of metal I had found in the old sailor's boat. In the moonlight it looked like a tooth.

"Thanks for helping us." I shouted at the ocean. There was no response. Happy as I was for being rescued, I had to admit he freaked me out. "Where did he come from?" I thought out loud.

"Probably jumped off the burning boat," Adam said.

"I doubt it. I don't want to think about it now."

"Where are we?" Adam asked.

"How do I know? Down shore somewhere. Follow me." I stumbled over some rocks; seaweed crunched under my feet. I stubbed my toe on a log. "Ow!" We took baby steps and I felt with my feet for dry sand.

"Wait for me," Adam said.

"Oh man, I'm right here." I felt for his hand.

We couldn't have gone more than three metres before the hard-packed sand became softer and warmer.

"Dry sand. We'll go up a bit higher and wait until morning...I'm zonked." I collapsed on my back, arms behind my head. On a clear night I could see a million stars dotting the sky. No such luck tonight.

"I'm pooped." Adam lay on his back beside me, his arms tucked under his head.

"You might even be cool someday." I gave Adam a little punch and he inched closer. "Hey, don't crowd me."

This wasn't exactly what I had planned for Adam's first day here. How was I supposed to know he couldn't swim very well? Despite my scrapes and bruises, I felt okay. The breeze would keep the mosquitoes from devouring us.

"Do you think that man will come back?" Adam asked.

"I hope not," I answered.

Right now I was more worried about Danny swimming to shore than the strangeness of the old sailor. It felt like days since we'd watched Danny dive into the water.

"I hope Danny's okay," I said. I swallowed the lump in my throat.

"He's kind of mean," Adam said.

"No, he's just like that, he's a good guy."

There was nothing I could do except settle into my bed of sand and wait until morning. My parents were going to kill me, but right now I'd wash a thousand dishes if it meant I could crawl into my warm bed.

I said a silent prayer for Danny.

Chapter 12

"**S**ophie!" a woman's voice called.

The brown dog zigzagged up the beach in that lopsided way of a sniffer.

I stood up and waved madly at the woman.

"Morning!" She breathed hard. Strands of wild grey hair sprung out from under her hat.

"We're lost," I said.

The woman reached for the dog's collar, but Sophie had already planted her front paws on Adam.

Adam groaned and sat up. "Whoa." He jumped to his feet.

"Down, Sophie." She smiled and gave us a good once-over. "Looks like you've been here all night."

"We have...well, most of it." I rubbed the dog's ears. "She's a lab."

"Yes, and a handful. You must be the boys from Fox Harbour." She looked down the empty beach. "How did you get here?"

"In a boat," I said. "Two boats."

"Two? Well, thank goodness you're all right. Heard on the radio folks are looking for you." She eyed me. "I'm Dot Hatfield. I used to work at the plant...you must be Matt, I can see your dad in you. And who's this young man?"

Adam stared at the woman. She wore a man's jacket and big rubber boots.

"My cousin Adam, he's visiting from Toronto," I said.

"Well, you're certainly getting the grand tour."

"What about Danny?" I asked.

"I don't know anything about a Danny," she said.

I felt sick. We began to pick our way over the dunes. They stood like small hills, hiding the house behind. It figures we slept so close to civilization and didn't know it.

"The ghost man saved us." Adam said.

"An old man...rowed us to shore, after our boat sank."

"He didn't talk and he looked really scary," Adam said.

"He rowed away before I could thank him...do you know who he is?"

"An old man?" She looked at us. "I'd say you're luckier than most."

Grey clouds blocked the morning sun. The dark sky looked like rain. The sea heaved up and down, making it too dangerous for even the toughest fishers to go out. There would be no boats today.

"You're cold, we must get you inside," Mrs. Hatfield said.

I followed her along the narrow path. Adam trailed behind, one hand on Sophie's back.

"Where are we?" I asked.

"Malagash. You boys travelled near ten kilometres. We'll call your folks, then get some food into you."

The wind blew steadily over the dunes, the sand stinging my bare legs. It took only five minutes to walk to the woman's house. It sat alone behind the dunes, a small house with peeling white paint and an old barn behind it. A sudden gust of wind pushed us toward the porch.

Mrs. Hatfield stopped and looked up at the darkening sky. "There's a nor'easter blowing in."

She opened the door and waved us in. I smelled the biscuits sitting on the large wood stove. Sophie went to her bed in the corner and lay on her side. "Poor girl, she's tired these days. She'll be a mother soon," Mrs. Hatfield said. The old kitchen had an iron pump beside the sink, and a scaredy cat that sprung off the counter and ran under the stove. Mrs. Hatfield lived alone.

She hurried across the room and picked up the phone. "What's your number?" she asked. I waited while she dialled. "John, it's Dot Hatfield. Good news...yes, both of them, on the beach, a bit sandy but they're fine. Here he is." Mrs. Hatfield waved me over.

"Dad," I swallowed. "Yes, we're okay...where's Danny?" I squeezed the phone with both hands and watched Mrs. Hatfield fill the kettle.

"Thank God you boys are all right." His voice sounded funny. "Danny's okay. At home getting some sleep." The knot in my stomach loosened.

"Why did he take so long?" I took a deep breath.

"We've all had a rough night...what's important is you're all right. We'll talk later—Maddy wants to speak to Adam."

I tried to focus on the fact that we were all safe. "Adam, phone."

I'd been cold for so many hours it was starting to feel like my natural state. The heat of the kitchen thawed my arms and legs, and I began to shake.

"Here." Mrs. Hatfield put a blanket around my shoulders.

"Thanks. My friend Danny's okay. He swam to shore last night. He was supposed to get help."

"Rough water last night," she said. The kettle started a high-pitched wail.

"But he took too long—we could've drowned." *All my worry about the close call we had, and Danny's in bed.*

"Everyone's safe, that's what's important." Mrs. Hatfield set mugs of hot chocolate on the table.

"Who's that?" I pointed to a photograph hanging above the kitchen table.

"That's my grandfather. He was a sailor."

"Is everyone here a sailor?" Adam put down the phone.

"Good heavens, no." Mrs. Hatfield motioned for us to sit. "At least, not nowadays. Granddad was lost at sea. Sailed on a three-masted schooner."

"Like the ghost man," Adam said as we sat down. "He rowed—"

I kicked Adam under the table.

My head hurt. Who was the sailor? Had we really seen a ship on fire last night? And how could Danny be home sleeping? He'd had time to swim to shore twice while Adam and I almost died. The wind shook the window. Outside, dark clouds moved across the sky.

Chapter 13

❦

I put my pen down and stared out our living room window. Empty lawn chairs slid across the deck. I didn't have time for outside, anyway.

"Put some lights on in here." Mom flicked the switch and came over to give me another hug.

"Yuck, Mom."

"I'm just glad you're safe. I hope we can find the man who rowed you ashore and thank him properly."

"Why is it called a nor'easter?" Adam pressed his nose to the glass.

"It's a storm from the northeast with waves three metres tall and wind that can push you over," I said. The window rattled. I looked outside and saw a yellow slicker blowing up the walk.

"Lordy, who's out in this weather?" Dad asked.

"I'll get it." The yellow slicker dripped in the doorway. "Danny." I blocked the doorway. My stomach churned.

"Hey. I wanted to see—"

"*Now* you show up."

"What?" Danny glared at me. "I almost drowned getting help."

"You almost *drowned*? We almost *died*. Why didn't you get help?"

"*Ocean Lad* was gone. I ran down the beach to the Millers's boat, but there weren't any oars."

"You could have got your dad—you were more worried about your own hide than my life."

Danny's face went red. "That's not true! I went to get Mitch, and we ran to your house, and your dad called the coast guard. We've been up all night."

"The water kept rising...Adam can't swim that far." My voice squeaked.

"You can't either," Danny said.

I stepped back like I'd been punched. My shoulders heaved up and down. Tears mixed with the rain pelting my face. "You were slow."

"And you shouldn't have let Adam go out."

"It was your idea." My voice cracked.

"No one twisted your arm." Danny stepped back out of the doorway and into the rain.

I slammed the kitchen door shut.

৩

"Emma's called twice," Dad said.

"I'll call her tomorrow." I focused on my potatoes. "I'm really tired." I pushed back my chair.

Catherine's door stood open. She laid on her side, eyes open and thumb in her mouth. I leaned over her crib. "I'll tell you what we did last night, but you have to promise not to tell." She popped her thumb out.

"We saw a ship on fire, an old one. A really old one. And an old man." She popped her thumb back in. "I can hardly believe it, but somehow I'm going to find out more.

For now, it's our secret. I'll get pictures of the ship and show everyone at school. What do you think about that?"

Catherine's eyes closed.

Back in my room, Adam lay curled on his mattress, his arm thrown over his teddy. I opened my dresser drawer. This morning I had stashed the tooth in one of my socks. Finally, I was alone and could check it out. It was pure gold, I was sure of it. I rubbed the smooth metal in my fingers then put it back.

I fell on my bed and stared at the ceiling. I thought of the sandbar—we'd had so much fun playing on it—but then I remembered the terror of just Adam and I crouched on the rock, watching the black water rise. I shivered.

Chapter 14

❦

"**O**cean Lad was buried at sea." Dad and I stood at the top of the cliff. The nor'easter had passed in the night, leaving a perfect day. The squawking seagulls chased the fishing boats.

"She was a good boat," Dad said stiffly.

"We shouldn't have gone out."

"We have rules for a reason. We trusted you to make sensible choices. We were beside ourselves. Whatever possessed you to take Adam out there?"

"I'm sorry." I blinked back tears. "There's something else…we saw a light on the water."

Dad looked at me blankly.

"A kind of a strange light."

"Probably one of the coast guard ships in the fog. I wish they'd seen you, we could've gotten you out of the water much earlier."

"Yeah, maybe." I decided to keep the rest to myself until I had a chance to investigate.

❦

Behind me the bushes swished, and I turned to see Adam.

"Where are you going?" Adam asked.

"Danny's."

"Oh." Adam squinted at the house on the other side of the barn. "Can I come?"

"May as well." I figured he would tag along anyway.

I took a deep breath and marched ahead.

Danny was bouncing a soccer ball around the lawn mower sitting in the tall grass.

"Hey," I said.

Danny gave the ball a hard kick and it bounced off the wall and almost took off my head. "Hey yourself."

"Come on, let's check out the beach." I looked around. "Something happened out there last night."

"Can't. My old man's really pissed. I have to cut the grass."

"I can help." I grabbed the rope and pulled hard. The machine gave an awful fart-like noise and blue smoke curled out the side.

Adam covered his ears.

"Never heard a lawn mower before?" Danny asked. "Forget it." He leaned against the side of the house.

"Don't take it out on him," I said. "It was bad, but wait till you hear."

"We saw an apparition," Adam said.

"A what?" Danny said.

"He means a ghost."

"Yeah right," Danny said.

I described the old sailor in the rowboat. He seemed less ghost-like now, an old guy who came along just in time. We were lucky.

"You could tell he wasn't real," Adam said.

"That's crazy," I said, but my heart lurched a little.

"How do you know that?" Danny asked.

"He didn't talk," Adam said. "Not even a sound."

"Maybe he just doesn't like to talk, or he can't," I said.

"He had on weird clothes." Adam jumped up and pulled his T-shirt loose. "All floaty and everything."

"What else?" Danny stood up straight.

"There's the burning ship," I said. I hadn't figured this out, and if Adam hadn't seen it too, I'd thought I dreamed it.

"It's best to leave it alone." Danny said. "You never know about these things."

"Don't mention this to anyone, okay? My parents are kind of freaked right now." I needed time to think this over and do some research. Besides, I didn't need my parents watching my every move. I needed to see it again.

"I wonder who the old man was?" Danny asked.

"Dunno." I fished around in my pocket. "But look." I showed Danny the gold tooth.

Chapter 15

❦

After supper, Adam and I rode our bikes on the packed dirt beside Main Street. We drove by the post office and two churches but had no time to stop at Mr. Boyle's gas station for Popsicles. Main Street was the only street in Fox Harbour with stores. It began with Johnson's Variety and ended with the fishermen's wharf. My favourite place for lunch was here: a bus painted white with two picnic tables outside. I liked the burgers best.

"Adam, come on, we're late," I called over my shoulder.

We were going to watch Danny's soccer team play Amherst. The field sat behind the high school and beside our little school. The yellow grass, worn out from summer, had died in the hard-packed clay. White chalk lines disappeared into the dust and fans argued the out of bounds. It seemed like most of the town had turned out; it was rumoured that our team would go to the provincials. We climbed up the rickety bleachers and squeezed onto the end. Emma sat behind us.

"Who's winning?" I asked.

"Two nothing for Fox Harbour." Emma answered. "Danny scored."

I looked at the guys on the bench, then tried to focus on the game. Danny charged in and butted the ball with his head, Roger took the pass and kicked it between the posts. Parents stomped and hollered.

"Three nothing and just thirty seconds left," I said.

"The probability of someone scoring now is zero."

"You must be Adam?"

"Yes."

"Emma." She stuck out her hand. "I go away for a day and miss all the fun. Were you scared? I want to hear everything."

The three of us leaned in together. I skipped over the hours in my sinking boat and got to the important part as the soccer game ended and players left the field. "The fog kept moving around, but I'm sure it was a ship." I kept my voice low.

"We killed them!" Danny was walking over the bleacher toward us, soccer cleats slung over his soaked jersey.

"Good game," Emma said, moving to make room on the bleachers. "Listen...a three-masted ship...on fire?"

"And a ghost," Adam said.

"Matt wants to investigate it," Danny said. "Don't tempt fate."

"Oh my god, it's the phantom ship." Emma grabbed my arm.

"That's just a tale," I said. "At least I thought it was."

"It sails in the Northumberland Strait. It's a ghost ship," Emma said excitedly.

"Shh! Let's keep it quiet, okay?" I looked around at the few people still sitting in the stands. "We need facts."

"I bet my grandfather will know," Danny said.

It had been three nights since we had been stranded on the water. It seemed less scary now that I was sitting here with my friends, and I liked being the one to tell about it.

"Tomorrow, let's meet at Danny's," I suggested.

"Yeah, bring your bikes, we'll go see my Gramp."

৻৵৩

Adam and I raced through the pile of pancakes Aunt Maddy made for breakfast the next day. I grabbed one more handful of blueberries and pushed back my chair.

"What are you boys up to today?" Aunt Maddy asked.

"We're going to Danny's," I said.

"You two are keeping busy, I've hardly seen you. Adam, let me know when you want to go for a swim."

"We're just riding our bikes...maybe we can stay at Matt's longer."

I shot Adam a look. I didn't want him giving Aunt Maddy any ideas as to what we were up to. We'd have to work fast if we wanted another chance to see the ship.

"I'm afraid not; school's starting soon," Aunt Maddy said.

When we got to Danny's, Emma was sitting on his lawn. A red bike stood on its kickstand.

"Is that yours?" I asked.

"Just got it."

"Cool."

"I outgrew my old one."

This I was well aware of; Emma now towered above me. She pulled her cap down low on her forehead. "Let's go."

Danny's grandfather's house was half a kilometre down shore. We pushed our bikes through a field until we reached the path that followed the shoreline. Single file we rode: Danny, Emma, me, and Adam.

Chapter 16

❦

Danny's grandfather lived alone in a tiny cottage on a cliff, as close to the sea as it could be without falling in. Last summer Danny and I watched a truck dump boulders over the cliff to stop the pounding waves from taking the cottage away. Today the sea was calm. We dropped our bikes and made our way around to the front of the house. Mr. Williams sat in his chair on the porch. His face had more lines than a road map, and his eyes were slits so tiny I sometimes wondered if he was sleeping. Lots of white hair covered his head. My dad said that Ed Williams would sit on his porch, looking at the sea, until he died. He loved the ocean and if he couldn't fish it, he would at least look at it.

"What's this? Company?" He pulled a pair of glasses out of his pocket. "Danny, you've brought some friends! Sit, sit." He gestured at us with his good arm. Since he was on the only chair, we sat down on the wood floor.

"Hi, Mr. Williams," Emma said.

"That Emma? Growing like a weed. And Matt, heard about your night at sea. Got to be careful, son. Who's this young'un?"

"My cousin Adam."

"Hello, sir." Adam stared at the empty shirt sleeve, folded up just below the elbow.

"Maddy's boy?" The old man peered over his glasses. "Been on the water too. She's in your blood, just like the rest of 'em."

"What—" Adam started.

"Gramps, we have a question."

"Just a second, let this young lad have his say."

"What...what happened to your arm?" Adam asked.

"Well, you see, I was out on the Strait and this great shark jumped clear out of the water, wanted all of me. I wasn't having none of that. Here's my arm, and I said 'enough!' and bludgeoned it with a harpoon."

We laughed at Adam's horrified face.

"Aw, Gramps. Don't pay any attention, Adam, he got it caught in the fishing tackle."

"Sea's a dangerous place." Mr. Williams shook his head.

"Tell us about the phantom ship," Danny said.

"The phantom ship? Where'd you hear about that?"

"We think we saw it," I added. I hardly ever saw Mr. Williams in town, so I was betting that our secret would be safe for now.

"It's a fact we did," Adam said. "And a ghost. Matt has his tooth."

I dug in my pocket and pulled out the wad of tissue I'd wrapped the tooth in.

"Let's see what you have there...hmm. I'd say that's gold. The owner will be hankering to get that back—might even come looking for it."

"Have you seen the ship?" Emma asked.

His chin dropped to his chest. A squawking seagull circled, then plunged headfirst into the sea to catch a squirming fish. Danny's grandfather thought for so long I thought maybe he'd forgotten the question. Then his good hand rubbed his knee and he stared at the ocean. "Saw her once. I was just a young man, late getting the traps in, and the sun had set."

"What did it look like?" Danny asked.

"We didn't want no trouble and kept our distance. She was a beauty, with magnificent masts, brilliant orange. Her glow lit up the sea all around. There was a strange stillness to her."

"That's it." Adam said. "That's what we saw."

"Did you see anyone?" Emma asked.

"It's a ship of fire, couldn't say for sure, but I don't reckon anyone could survive that. Some folks say it's the light, kind of like them lights up north."

"The Aurora Borealis," Adam said.

"We don't need Wikipedia, we've got you." Danny slapped Adam on the back.

I looked at Adam. To my surprise, Danny and Emma didn't seem to mind having him around. I inched closer to Mr. Williams. "What about the old sailor?"

"Careful son, don't want to be stirring things up...them sailors may have unfinished business."

"What kind of business?" Danny asked.

"Let the dead be."

"How come you never told me about the phantom ship before?" Danny asked.

"Lots of ships go down, sailors are a superstitious bunch...best leave it alone."

A chill climbed up my spine. Wind flattened the sea grass; the tide had shifted, moving back to shore. We watched the horizon; the gentle waves were hypnotizing.

No one spoke for a while. I didn't want to be rude, but we had things to do. I nudged Emma.

"Wow, thanks so much, Mr. Williams. We have to be going now," Emma said.

"It's incredible, right here on the Northumberland Strait," I said. "Thanks, Mr. Williams."

"Yeah, thanks Gramps." Danny shook his hand.

"Bye." Adam waved from his bike.

We pedalled down the dirt road and clouds of dust, like ghosts, chased us. At Danny's yard we dropped our bikes.

"We have to find the phantom ship," Emma said.

My heart skipped a beat. Who knew how long the ship would stay around our shore? Besides, it was almost September and the weather was sure to turn.

"This week," I said.

Chapter 17

❦

We bunched together at one end of Emma's kitchen. Stacks of books and paper teetered near her computer. I watched, as if staring at the screen would make the window open faster. Emma and Adam sat at the desk; Adam worked the mouse while Emma pointed at a list of websites. "There, there," she said. Danny and I leaned in.

"I don't know why you kids aren't playing outside," Emma's mom said.

I knew she didn't really mind. She had put oatmeal cookies with chocolate chips on nice plates and poured everyone a glass of lemonade.

"Almost done, Mom," Emma said. "Just a project about the ocean."

"Projects, this time of year? Well, I'll be in the garden... at least *I'll* enjoy this lovely weather."

"Thanks, Mrs. Miller," I said. I said a silent prayer of thanks for the nice weather. My dad would otherwise be pulling up a chair at the mention of a project.

"Those are the wrong ships," I said. I wondered about my sanity. Had the fire been real? Had anyone other than Adam, who'd been just as exhausted and dehydrated as me, seen the sailor? Or had we just dreamed him up? There had to be a logical explanation, but then I put my fingers on the tooth in my pocket.

"Just type in 'phantom ship,'" Emma said to Adam.

"Needs to be more precise," Adam said. He typed in "Phantom Ship, Northumberland Strait."

"Hey, there are three websites," Danny said. "'Tall Ships,' 'Ship of Fire,' and 'Ghost Encounters.'"

My heart banged against my ribs. I stared at a drawing on the screen by one of the links. "That's it!" I pumped my fist into the air. "I knew it." Adam clicked and the burning ship filled the screen.

"Listen." Emma began to read: *"A ship of fire, a three-masted square-rigger with fire on every rope."*

"We told you it was real," Adam said.

"There's more," Emma said: *"One tale goes that the ship was occupied by pirates who had made a pact with the devil. The ship was about to sink, so the pirates let the devil hide their treasure; in exchange for this favour, the pirates had to sail forever on the burning ship."*

"Man, pirate treasure," Danny said. "And ghosts."

"Hidden treasure," I said.

I looked out the window. A long way out, the sea looked dark blue. Mrs. Miller was tying her tomato plants to the stakes stuck in the ground.

"Shh." Emma read on: *"There have been several attempts to reach the ship but none have been successful."*

"Never?" Sweat rolled down between my shoulder blades. Was it possible to reach the phantom ship? It'd have to be at night. Then a thought paralyzed me: *maybe the ship had reached us.*

"We have to find it first," Danny said.

"We could get close enough to take a picture," Adam said, then stuttered. "Uh-oh, this could be a problem: *'The phantom ship is seen just before a strong easterly wind, indicating a storm approaching.'*"

"We don't want to get caught in that," I said. I didn't want them to think I was a chicken, but seriously, this could get dangerous.

"Aw, we just had a storm, what are the chances?" Danny said.

"Exactly—we just had a storm," I said.

"Timing is everything," Adam said. "And a safe boat." He looked pointedly at me.

"Right," Emma said. "The weather's good. I say we go tomorrow night; that will give us a day to get ready."

"I'm in," Danny said right away.

"We'll need to make a list," Adam grabbed a piece of scrap paper from the teetering pile.

Emma had a solid boat, and we'd have life jackets, a flashlight, drinkable water, and a good crew.

"Our parents will never let us go," I reminded them.

"You can't tell them," Danny said.

"We go out in my boat all the time; it'll just be for a few hours," Emma insisted.

"Well, Adam shouldn't go," I said. I had enough to worry about and I had seen his attempt at swimming—not that we planned to get wet.

"What? There's no way I'm missing this." He stood with Emma and Danny and looked right into my eyes without blinking.

"We're a team." Danny put his big paw on Adam's shoulder.

I had to admit Adam was winning them over, but still, I didn't appreciate the fact he got us stuck that night.

ॐ

I burst to the surface, my lips round like a fish sucking its last drop of air. My legs kicked the black water. Its grip tightened. *No!* I screamed. The icy tentacles pulled panic over me like a blanket. My eyes opened, the pounding of my heart reminded me I was still alive.

The blankets twisted around my ankles. My skin still had the creepy feel of the octopus's touch. Gradually, the dream let go and pushed to the corner of the room.

A stick was propping open the window and the curtains were moving in the breeze. I lay on my mangled bed and gazed at the same stars as the sailors. I took deep breaths and waited for my heartbeat to return to normal. Adam was sleeping on his back, arms thrown out wide. I was getting used to him hanging around, but he'd better not slow us down tomorrow.

In my head I made a list of the pros and cons. It was just a boat ride, no big deal. Emma had a good boat, the weather was good, and we might see the phantom ship. It would be an adventure. But we had to sneak out, and I could get in really big trouble. I should have felt bad about this but I didn't—and *that's* what made me feel bad.

Chapter 18

❧⌒❧

Adam got to breakfast first. While I waited for the comics, I read the headline LOW LOBSTER CATCH WORRIES FISHERMEN.

"Hey, don't hog the Cheerios," I said.

"And save some for me." Dad sat down with Catherine in his arms.

I'd decided mornings were the best times for babies. I patted down Catherine's puffs of red hair. She was happy like a clown. I offered her a Cheerio and she grabbed my fingers. We stared at each other for a moment, and I really thought she knew what I was up to.

"Here." I refilled my juice and poured some for Dad.

"Just saw Emma heading to the beach, had her oars... what are you boys up to today?"

Adam gagged on a mouthful of cereal. He pounded his chest and gulped some juice. "Excuse me."

I kept my eyes glued to my cereal. "Later we're going to the beach."

"Supposed to be a scorcher, I'll try to get away early—we can all take a swim."

"Good morning." The screen door banged behind Mom and Aunt Maddy. They had on their walking shoes and

Mom was wearing those striped pants I really hated, but I decided to be diplomatic and say nothing. "Nice track suit, Aunt Maddy."

"Why, thank you, Matt. Saw your friend Emma."

Jeez, did everyone see Emma today? It had been a whole week since our night on the water and I still felt like I was under constant surveillance.

"We'll all go to the beach later," Dad said.

"Too bad you can't take the whole day off," said Mom.

"We have bills to pay...boys, wait until I'm back."

Adam ducked his head down and stuffed a second slice of toast into his mouth. At that moment, Catherine decided to grab Dad's glass. The orange juice ran across the table like a wave, circling Adam's bowl, and creeping forward until it poured over the edge of the table. *Thank you, Catherine.* Springing into action, I grabbed the super-absorbent paper towels and laid them one by one over the mess.

"Darn. John, you know she'll grab anything." Mom reached for the dishtowel. Adam leaped from the table.

"Whoops! Come on, little lady, I'll get you some clean clothes." Dad made his escape.

Mom and I wiped up the linoleum floor. I loaded the dishwasher and put the cereal away.

"Thanks, honey. Could you do one more thing? Would you return a library book for me?"

"Sure, no problem." I wanted to keep busy, but couldn't be too helpful or it would be weird.

"Here." Dad put Catherine in her playpen and pulled a toonie out of his pocket. "Stop by the store and get yourself a Popsicle."

"Thanks." I put the money in my pocket and grabbed my knapsack off its hook and stuffed in Mom's library book: another boring story about the queen of England.

I went into the living room, where Adam was sitting at the computer. "Want to bike to the library?"

"I'll stay here, I'm checking the tidal charts."

"Be careful," I mouthed. He was definitely a computer nerd, but he had been finding some very useful information.

♋

I pushed my bike into the driveway and jumped on. I pedalled as fast as I could, but that lump in my stomach stayed with me. I knew Emma had a sturdy boat, and Danny and Emma were sailors, and if we could get a picture we would have bragging rights. I also knew we could land in a pile of trouble. It was like standing on the highest diving platform at the wharf: one moment I couldn't wait, and the next I was terrified. It made me want to vomit. I couldn't back out. I'd already said I was in. I kept pedalling.

I sailed into Mrs. MacDonald's yard, the back wheel of my bike kicking up bits of gravel. I dropped the bike to the ground and followed the path around to the back of the house.

The town library was pretty pathetic, just one room. The typewritten note taped to the door gave the hours. Thursdays, closed. I pulled Mom's hardcover book out of my knapsack, the royal family posed on the cover. I opened the metal slot and peered in. Two books lay in the basket under the door. I got down so that my eyes lined up with the slot and my nose was in danger of being snapped off. One book lay upside down, but the other one stared at me.

Holy cow.

There was a picture of a three-masted schooner on the front. Ancient, with ratty sails. A detective doesn't believe in coincidences.

Chapter 19

❧

I peeled back the sticky paper on my grape Popsicle and dropped it into the overstuffed garbage can.

"Not at the shore today?" Mr. Boyle sat on his stool behind the counter.

Boyle's General Store carried just about everything our town might need: thin rope, thick rope, hooks, and buckets lined one wall. Boxes of spearmint gum crowded the display of lotto tickets, lined up in neat rows under glass. The drink cooler had little rivers of water running down its glass doors.

"Just doing an errand for Mom." I took another bite of Popsicle and licked the purple juice from my fingers.

"You boys had half the town looking for you."

"Yeah, it was kind of scary."

"Saw Danny go by earlier, he had his soccer ball. A bit hot for that, eh?" He mopped his head with a giant blue hanky. Mr. Boyle came to the soccer games when Mrs. Boyle could watch the store. Sometimes he gave the team free juice. "Hope to get the boat out later."

I shifted my weight from one foot to the other. "Did you ever hear about a phantom ship?"

"Sure, heard of her—never seen her, though."

"I was wondering if it's real, or, you know, just some story." I bit off a chunk of melting Popsicle.

"Well, all I know is that some fellas say they've seen her on the horizon. Haven't heard mention of her in a long time, though." Mr. Boyle cut the cord off a stack of newspapers with his jackknife. "Why you ask?"

"Nothing, just wondering." At least no one had been hurt—or worse, disappeared. "Thanks. I've got to go." I pushed the flip-top of the garbage can open and dropped my Popsicle stick in. Then I ran down the steps and crashed into a woman getting out of a truck parked at the curb. Her frizzy grey hair stood out in all directions: the woman who had found Adam and me on the beach.

"Mrs. Hatfield."

"Hello, Matt. My, you're in a hurry."

"Hi. I didn't know you shopped here."

"Well, I don't always venture this far, but an old neighbour moved over this way. Needed a bit of help getting some groceries, dropping off a few library books, that kind of thing."

All those little hairs on the back of my neck suddenly stood up. *I bet that book on ships was hers.* I'd have to be very careful not to give it away.

"Thanks for your help the other day."

"I'm glad I was there." She made no sign of moving.

I took a breath. This was the only person I knew who lived near the spot where the old sailor had dropped us off.

"Could I ask you something?"

"What would you like to know?" She studied my face.

"Have you ever seen the phantom ship?"

Her mouth opened in surprise. She folded her arms against her body.

"No, I haven't. My grandfather was quite obsessed. He spent many a night watching the sea, even ventured out at night...until...one night he didn't come home."

A chill crawled up my spine. "What do you mean?"

Mrs. Hatfield sighed.

"No one knows. My grandmother almost went crazy with the waiting. He was lost at sea like so many others." She fixed me with a look.

"What about his boat?"

"Never appeared. It was like the sea just swallowed him and that little dory up."

"Dory?"

"Oh, they all used them back then." Then her eyes came back to the present, and I knew that was all I was going to get. "Never mind, water under the bridge. Don't hear much about the ship anymore."

"We saw some kind of light when we were out there the other night."

"Oh, things look different at night."

I studied the ground. Of course. It was just light reflecting on the water. We had been cold and tired and hungry. A hallucination. But Adam had seen it too, and it was just like in the picture. I swallowed the words before I confessed to her that we were planning to find it.

"Yeah, that's probably it...nice to see you, I've got to go."

"You kids be careful out there."

I got on my bike and pedalled hard to the soccer field. What did she mean by that? Did her grandfather have an accident, or find the phantom ship? Or both?

Chapter 20

❦

I stood on my pedals and jumped over the holes in the parking lot. Danny's teammates were getting on their bikes. Red dirt covered their jerseys. Cleats swung from the handlebars. I half-lifted one hand when they passed. I straddled my bike and watched as the slowpoke goalie was the last to disappear down the road.

On the other side of the field, Coach Dale was spreading white chalk where the lines should be. Danny's bike was leaning against the equipment room, and the door stood half open. I heard a bump and stepped into the doorway. There was one window on the east side. A line of sun ran over a rack of balls, across the floor, and onto the stack of filing cabinets. Danny was on his knees there. He wiggled the bottom drawer back and forth. He stopped, glanced at the window, then went back to fighting with it.

This was Coach Dale's domain.

Danny shuffled through some papers, then pulled out a fat, letter-sized envelope. He took off the elastic and pulled out a wad of bills. I held my breath. He put the bills back in the envelope and shoved it into his pocket. I was already backing out the door. I did nothing.

"Oh!" Danny jumped. He filled the doorway. "Jeez, where'd you come from?"

For a minute I couldn't say anything. "I was running an errand, and I saw your bike." I was looking over his shoulder.

"Wait up, I just have to see Coach." He ran across the field. They talked a minute, Danny with his back to me, hands in his pockets. Coach slapped him on the shoulder and Danny faked a punch. Man, he acted so normal.

⚭

Adam and I dropped our towels by Dad and ran across the hot sand to Emma's red and white umbrella. She was balancing a book on her legs, her extra large sunglasses like bug eyes. She shut the book and shoved it into her beach bag.

"A perfect day," Emma said.

"Yeah...just perfect."

"What's wrong with you?"

"He's grouchy," Adam said.

"I am not." I threw my towel down and jumped on it before I scorched my feet. Maybe I should have told someone. But we needed Danny for tonight.

"Make some room for me." Adam spread his towel in the bit of shade left.

"Let's walk." Emma looked at her mother fanning herself.

"I'll get Danny," Adam said. Danny was a hundred metres up the beach, putting another rock on our wharf.

The tide was halfway out. We could follow the shore for a kilometre, moving sandbar to sandbar, and the water would never reach our knees.

The four of us walked side by side. Adam had been here for a week and already the T-shirt lines on his arms had disappeared. His keen interest in science and a year in Boy Scouts had paid off. He'd shown me his compass-reading abilities, and just maybe he could help pull the oars.

We stepped off the beach into the water. Wet sand squished between my toes. Every pore of my body sucked in the salt. Sandpipers ran across the sandbar.

"Meet at my boat by midnight," Emma said.

"I'll bring my compass," Adam said.

"Good. The life jackets and oars will be in the boat." Emma kicked through the shallow water.

"I've got a flashlight," Danny said.

"Yeah, make sure it works," I said. I hadn't forgotten how dark it had been.

"Don't forget water and snacks, and I'm bringing my camera," Adam said.

"I can bring the snacks," Danny said.

"I'll bring my own," I said.

"What's wrong with you?" Emma jabbed me in the ribs.

"Yeah, something's eating you. You going to chicken out?" Danny said.

"Hey, I'm no chicken."

Emma gave me a look. "Right, everyone bring a water bottle and snack."

Danny plopped down and stuck his legs in the water. "What if we don't find it? Could be a wild goose chase."

"Maybe we won't," I said.

"Okay, Mr. Negative, but what if we do?" Emma sat down by Danny.

"We could be rich!" Adam shouted.

"We don't know for sure if it's real. Besides, it's not about the money." I lay down beside Adam and put my

DEBORAH TOOGOOD

hands behind my head. Fluffy white clouds drifted across the blue sky.

"Who says?" Danny said.

"I checked the weather, tonight looks good," said Adam.

"And tomorrow?" I asked.

"Something's coming in in a few days, kind of unpredictable with wind currents and everything." Adam looked at the horizon.

My stomach lurched. Hadn't there been something about a sighting just before a storm?

We didn't say much walking back up the beach. Dad had set up the umbrella. I fell into one of the chairs.

"Want some help?" Adam squatted down by Catherine and began to dig a hole.

Dad sat the cooler in the shade. "Call Danny and we'll all go for a swim."

"He's busy." I pulled off my T-shirt and ran for the water.

Chapter 21

❧~❧

"I'm beat." I yawned, got off the couch, and stretched again.

"What, no snack?" Mom looked up from her book.

"I think I'll just go to bed." I had already stashed my water bottle and three granola bars under my bed.

Dad was watching a news show on TV. I'd been trying to avoid the footage of a ship heaving in heavy water. A helicopter hovered over it with rescue lines swinging wildly in the air.

"That's not my cup of tea," Dad said.

"Me neither." Adam slid off the couch.

"All that swimming wear you two out?" Aunt Maddy asked.

"I'm not far behind," Dad yawned. "Pleasant dreams."

"Night," I said with a little wave.

I climbed the stairs with lead feet. I brushed my teeth extra long, then tried to grin at myself in the mirror. It looked more like a mug shot. Adam slid under his blanket wearing his shorts and T-shirt, his compass tucked in his pocket. I set the alarm for 11:45 P.M. and placed it under my pillow, not that I'd be able to sleep.

"Sure you want to come?" I asked.

"Yes, I want to see the phantom ship again."

"Aren't you scared?"

"It won't be like last time. We're prepared, and we have Emma and Danny."

I hadn't expected Adam to take so well to our adventure, and I had almost forgiven him for getting us stuck on the sandbar. What surprised me the most was that I didn't mind him tagging along.

"I almost forgot." I slipped out of bed and opened the top drawer of my dresser. I dug around for the gold tooth; my hand grabbed the cool metal, and I put it in my pocket. Adam had already conked out.

I tossed in the dark and waited for sleep. All day I had tried to keep my thoughts from going back to the equipment room. The creak of the drawer, Danny holding the pack of bills, and his casual manner with Coach. It was like a bad movie. There had been a lot of fundraisers lately; Coach must have put the money there during practice. And now I felt like an accomplice. Why would Danny need money? It didn't make sense. But what if we found the phantom ship? If there were pirates, there might be treasure. We could put the money back and no one would know.

Chapter 22

❧❧

The alarm under my pillow shook me awake. Eleven forty-five. Getting out of my warm bed and going out on the water didn't seem quite so appealing now. Either way, there would be consequences. I rolled over and looked at Adam curled on his mattress. I could sneak out and let him be, but he was our guy on the compass. Besides, he would kill me if I didn't wake him.

"Adam." I shook his shoulders.

"What?"

"Shh!" I put my hand over his mouth. "Oh, gross." Snot dribbled out of his nose. I wiped my hand on his blanket.

"Allergies." He wiped his nose, then stuffed a fistful of tissues into his pocket.

I grabbed my supplies and signalled him to follow me. The door to my room opened soundlessly. Outdoor noises floated in the open windows; tonight the frogs at the Sullivans' pond were competing with the screeching crickets. Dad snored, which I considered a good sign.

We tiptoed down the hall. The greatest challenge would be the fourth step. We would have to skip over it—unless we wanted a loud creak echoing through the house. More signals to Adam.

First step, I wished Adam wouldn't breathe so loud.

Second step, I wondered if the others had changed their minds.

Third step, I lunged over the fourth step and had just placed my foot on the fifth step when Catherine cried out.

We froze.

Silence.

The steady ticking of our grandfather clock reminded me to get moving.

Six, seven, eight, nine, ten, the hum of the refrigerator guided us to the kitchen. The room looked foreign. The screen door would be the last barrier, impossible to open without noise. I put my hand on the door as if I were defusing a bomb. It opened an inch. The high-pitched creak vibrated through the house. There was no stopping now. With the door just wide enough to squeeze through, we were out. My trembling hands fastened the door shut, sealing my family safely inside.

Moonlight dotted the yard. The shadows of trees criss-crossed on the grass. No need to put on our sweaters; the August night had stayed warm. We would follow the road.

త

Each step, every breath of night air, filled us with excitement. Soon we were running.

"Did you hear Catherine? I thought for sure we'd get caught," I said.

"Yeah, and your Dad's snores." Adam sucked in a lungful of air and snorted it out.

We both burst out laughing.

"Matt," Adam said.

"Yeah?"

"This is the best thing that's ever happened to me."

I grinned. "Maybe you can come back next year."

Enough moonlight filtered through the trees that we could follow the road and not fall headfirst into the ditch. Our run slowed to a fast walk. I avoided the spookiness of the woods. Suddenly, an awful shriek pierced the darkness. Then another.

"What's that?" Adam whispered.

More shrieks. A battle.

"Wild turkeys," I said. They lived in the woods, and sometimes on summer nights I heard the squabbling. We began to run. Listening from my bed it didn't seem so bad, but out here was another thing.

"You're kidding," Adam panted beside me.

"I'm not. Danny's grandfather said years ago there was a turkey farm near here, and some of the turkeys still live in the woods."

"Turkeys can fly," Adam offered.

"Where do you get this stuff?"

"I read it."

"Stop," I said. "Here's the path to the beach."

We stepped into the salt air. After the gloom of the woods, the beach looked like daylight. Moonlight poured onto the water. Ripples brushed the sand. A perfect night.

"We're safe," Adam said.

"And here's the boat." The dory was larger than *Ocean Lad*. There were two seats across and a small one in the bow. A solid rope, attached to the anchor, lay half-buried in the sand, and a bailer lay in the bottom. Just as Emma promised, the life jackets had been stowed under the seats, and two oars lay beside them. I tucked my knapsack under the rear seat and sat on the gunnel, my legs dangling outside the boat.

I jumped at the crunch of footsteps on the bank.

"I thought Dad would never turn out the lights," said Emma.

"Two minutes to midnight. Where's Danny?" Adam asked.

"He'll be here." Danny wouldn't miss this, and I hated to admit it, but I didn't want to go out there without him.

"He's late," Adam said.

"Five minutes either way won't make a difference," said Emma.

"Can't he tell time?" I said.

"What's the matter?" Emma asked. "Something's bugging you. You keep picking on Danny."

I wanted to cough up the whole story, but I shrugged. "Nothing."

"Maybe his dad hasn't gone to bed yet," Adam said.

"If he doesn't come by twelve fifteen we'll go without him, okay?" Emma said.

We sat down on the side of the boat to wait.

"Ten after twelve," Adam said after a few minutes.

Maybe he'd been caught sneaking out, or hurt his ankle jumping from his bedroom window. Anxiety replaced my agitation. I really wanted him there.

"Well, it's a calm night, easy enough to row. You guys take that side."

Slowly I followed Emma's directions. We began to tug the boat toward the water.

"Someone's coming," Emma said. We ducked behind the boat—it wasn't like people ever strolled along the beach this time of night.

I knew that step. "It's Danny."

"All set." Danny unwrapped a flashlight from his sweatshirt. "We won't need this if the moon stays out." He stashed it under the seat. "It's waterproof. Hey, you going without me?"

"You're late," Adam said.

"Yeah, well, we're all here now." I heard the relief in my own voice.

I looked around. We'd tied our sweatshirts around our waists and put old sneakers on our bare feet—our usual boat stuff, minus sunglasses and baseball hats.

"What are we waiting for?" Danny grabbed one side of the dory. "Let's find that ship."

"Wait, put on your life jackets," Emma said.

"Aw, it's like a lake out there," Danny complained.

"Those are the rules." Emma began to hand out jackets.

No one had to tell Adam and me twice. Danny shrugged and pulled on the jacket, ignoring the fasteners in front. I kicked off my sneakers.

"Throw your shoes in the boat; we don't want anyone to find them and think we're swimming," Emma said. I did.

Danny and Adam stood on one side of the boat, and Emma and I took the other.

"One, two, three, lift," Emma said.

We began the march across the sand, our bright orange jackets like a uniform. Our feet reached the tiny waves. Together we lowered the boat into the shallow water.

"Everyone get in." Danny held the boat.

I took the middle seat and slid the oars into the oar-locks, happy to have something solid to hold onto. Adam parked himself on the narrow seat in the bow, and Emma sat in the stern. Danny gave a final shove and hopped in. The boat lurched, Emma moved over, and Danny plunked down opposite me.

I looked at the open ocean, the moonlight cutting a path like a highway across the water. If there was a ship of fire out there tonight, we'd see it.

Adam studied his compass.

"Thataway." He pointed to the northeast.

Chapter 23

❧

I understood why men went to sea. Being out here at night felt like time had stopped; we floated in our own world. Darkness closed in on three sides. The shoreline, my point of reference, looked grey and blurry, the usual markers gone. The sky was a canopy dotted with stars. I pulled back hard on the oars and the boat cut through the water, the shoreline shrinking. Each pull lifted my worry about Danny and propelled me closer to the phantom ship.

I rowed steady, following Adam's direction. A serious navigator for our little ship, he sat high on the bow. Danny sprawled on his seat opposite me, adding knots to the bailer's rope. Emma stared at the ocean. The quiet night sat on everyone, and we were content to listen to the steady dipping of the oars.

"What time is it?" I asked.

"Twelve-thirty," Danny said. "Want me to take over?"

"Not yet." I didn't mind the ache creeping into my shoulders.

"Suit yourself."

I had to push the picture of Danny on the soccer field out of my mind and focus on finding the phantom ship. We needed Danny onside—besides, I'd known him my whole life, and he just didn't do stuff like that. It didn't add up.

"Look." Adam pointed out to sea and brought my attention back to the present. I had to get a grip. In the distance I could see lights moving steadily across the water.

"It's a ship," Emma said.

A shipping lane ran between Prince Edward Island and Nova Scotia's mainland. It was common to see freighters at night. Even in daylight, fishers steered clear of these lanes—a ship could demolish a small boat. Tonight, I couldn't tell if it was one of our local salt ships or a mega-ship loaded with containers from Europe. Mesmerized, we watched the ship move away until the lights were no more than specks on the ocean and we were alone again.

Danny fumbled under the seat and pulled out his flashlight. He turned to face Adam and began flicking the light on and off. "Anyone know Morse code?"

"Danny." Emma reached for the light.

"Turn it off," I said. We didn't need to attract attention.

"Jeez, relax. This is boring," Danny sighed.

"I know some Morse code," Adam said, "from Scouts."

"Like what?" Danny asked.

"Like SOS. It's three short dots, three long dots, three short dots."

"Cool." Danny's fingers tapped it out on the seat. "You never know."

"It's for emergencies," Adam said. "It means 'save our souls.'"

Our boat slowed. My arms seized up. Rowing four people for an hour wasn't easy.

"Your turn," Emma said to Danny.

I'd made little progress since the freighter. I slid over and joined Emma in the stern. We sat forward, facing Danny, Adam's back to us. Danny dug the oars into the water and with a strong pull we surged forward.

"I heard you guys made the playoffs," Emma said.

"Yeah, I think we can go all the way to Halifax for the provincials." replied Danny.

"I guess the team has to raise some money," I said.

"We're almost there."

"How much do you need?" I wanted a big hand to clamp over my mouth, because I couldn't seem to control myself.

"Dunno. Coach said maybe we'll have a car wash on Saturday."

"Hey, we're getting off course," Adam said. He pointed northeast. Danny held one oar deep into the water, and the boat turned away from the shore. I watched the lights shrink. The stone in my gut was back.

"It's getting hazy," Adam said.

"It's the fog," I said. "The air's getting colder." Wisps of fog moved over the water, circling our boat and making it hard to see.

"I did a project on fog; you get it here because of the salt water." Adam said. "Waves shoot bits of salt into the air and condensation forms on the particles. The cooler night air helps, because there's not so much difference between the air and water temperatures."

"Cool, I didn't know that," Emma said.

"Yeah, I'll be sure to put that in my next project." Danny continued to pull us through the fog. The little boat lifted up and down as steady as a ticking clock.

"Shh, listen," hissed Emma.

At first I heard nothing, and then the hum of a boat cruising across the water. I looked around for the telltale light, but there wasn't even a shadow of a boat.

"We're not alone," Danny whispered.

The boat's engine chugged at low speed, then cut out altogether.

"They're up to something," Emma said.

"Shh." Adam signalled for us to be quiet.

The sound of water slapping against the hull of the mystery boat got louder. Danny pulled the oars in, and we crouched in our seats, holding our breath as the boat approached us. A cloud drifted over the moon, and like smoke, fog swirled around. The murmur of men's voices carried across the water. My hand crept up to check the fasteners on my life jacket. The other boat stayed on course. I gripped my seat. I heard a thud, then another. A shadow fell over our boat. Two men appeared in the back of a fishing boat.

"Whew. That was a close call." Emma puffed air out of her cheeks.

"They're pulling up traps," I said.

"Idiot poachers. I hope they get caught," Danny said.

"I think we would've seen the phantom ship by now," Adam's voice trembled slightly.

Emma glanced at her watch. "It's almost one thirty."

"Aw, come on, we've hardly looked." Danny picked up the oars.

"Why not look until two?" Emma suggested.

"I don't think it's out here tonight." I didn't like the fact that the lights on shore were barely pinpoints, that we were sharing our space with poachers, or that the water now had a small chop—a fact I'd been trying to ignore.

"Hey, you're the one who got us out here with stories of your phantom ship," Danny accused.

"They're not stories."

"We saw it," Adam insisted.

"I didn't make you come," I reminded Danny.

"Yeah, well, we're here now, and I'm not giving up like some scaredy cat."

"Stop it," Emma orderd. "Two o'clock. We'll stay until two."

"Fine." I looked down at the floor of the boat, my fists squeezed into tight balls. I wished with all my might it would appear right now, just to show them, so I could say "told you so." The ocean looked a dangerous black; not even the stars were shining.

"At least the poachers' boat is going in the opposite direction." Adam held up his compass. "We're off course, we should be going that way."

Danny yanked back on the oars and we moved forward. Our course put us into a light wind, and small waves began to slap against the bow. Adam leaned over the side, his hand trailing in the water, salt spray soaking his hair. Danny's breath came in short gasps. He pulled back a notch.

"The wind's up," Emma said. "Move over." She grasped one oar and braced her bare feet against the floor. "Pull." Danny followed Emma's lead, and together they steered our boat through the waves.

Ten minutes passed before Danny groaned, "Whew." He rested the oar in his lap. He'd been at it for almost an hour.

"I'll take over." I felt wimpy for suggesting we turn back.

Danny let the oar rest in the oarlock. "Sea's coming up."

"Whoa." Adam sat down hard on his seat.

"Stay down or we'll be fishing you out," Emma said.

She used her oar as a rudder, trying to keep us on course. I flopped down beside her. The glass-like surface was long gone, and the boat was rocking with the waves. We drew back on the oars; the boat inched forward.

DEBORAH TOOGOOD

"Not so easy, is it?" Danny asked. He sat in the stern facing us, arms crossed and legs out.

"It's not so bad." I tried not to pant. With the headwind, I wondered if we were moving at all.

"The weather channel didn't predict this," Adam said.

"Hard to call the weather out here," Emma said. The muscles popped on her forearms.

"Hey, what did you read about the phantom ship and the wind?" I asked Adam.

"It's seen before a storm," he replied.

"Out of the northeast," I added.

"That's where we're headed." Adam looked at his compass.

Danny sat up. "I'm not getting caught in no storm."

A storm hadn't been forecast. *Maybe the phantom ship created the rough sea.* My heart thumped faster. *If we could just stay out a bit longer—*

"That's it, two o'clock." Adam sounded relieved.

"We gotta get out of here," Danny said.

I slapped my oar down into the water. We couldn't stay out in rough seas, but I'd wanted a chance to show Danny and Emma. This was like being ahead the whole game and then losing with a minute to go. It wasn't fair. I felt the gold tooth in my pocket.

Slowly, I lifted my oar out of the water and let Emma turn the boat.

"Don't worry, we'll try again," she said.

"Maybe." I answered.

Now we were moving with the current, and soon the lights on shore grew brighter.

The buoy, marking the channel, clanged a greeting.

Danny gasped. "Oh, crap."

The hum of a fishing boat drifted toward us. Then the hull pushed out of the fog.

"Not them again," Adam said.

"Turn to starboard!" Emma cried.

Our boat detoured out to sea.

Chapter 24

❧

The waves thumped against the bow of the boat, and again our progress was slow. Clouds obliterated the moon; the sea was an inky black, the sky dark grey. I was hopeless on the oars. The wet from the seat soaked through my shorts.

I was completely miserable. A few days ago I was dreaming about treasure—or at the very least, ghost pirates. What had I dragged my friends into? *Fighting with the sea at night and hiding from poachers? I must be crazy.*

Emma and I pulled back on the oars, struggling to stay together. "I think it's safe now to head in," she said.

"Yeah, this is crazy, we're chasing ghosts." Danny slumped in the stern.

"Listen, what's that?" Emma hissed.

I smelled the diesel fuel at the same time I heard them. I could tell by the pitch of their voices that they were excited.

"It's the poachers' boat," Adam cried.

"How'd they find us?" Emma shoved her oar down and our boat slowed.

They hadn't.

I felt the shift in the light, first on my back, then on our boat, like someone moving a dimmer switch slowly up. My knees almost buckled.

"Holy crap," Danny said.

I whipped around to face the bow. A massive orange glow hung over the water, throwing a murky light on us. Three masts towered out of the mist. The ship appeared to hover on the water. No one moved on board. I stood, ignoring the tilt of our boat, the oars dangling from the oarlocks, my mouth hanging open. I thought I might faint.

The great ship rose in front of us, just like I'd said.

"Wow! I've got to get a picture." Adam dug into his knapsack, pulled out his camera, and kneeled on the little seat in the bow.

"It's real. The phantom ship is real," Emma murmured.

The utter amazement of my shipmates was enough. The ship lit up like the setting sun, a big red ball radiating light over the water. The waves pushed us closer. I saw flames leap off the rigging, but I felt no heat. Small hairs on my neck stood up. I grabbed the oars and jammed them straight down in the water. Our boat slowed.

"What are you doing?" Danny shouted.

"We're close enough." This was an old wooden schooner; nothing like this had sailed in our waters for a long time. I stared at the fiery ball. I had talked everyone into coming here and I didn't want them to get hurt because of me.

"What? What are we here for? No one's on it." Danny wrenched the other oar from my hand and began to propel us forward. The phantom ship loomed overhead. I made a lunge for the oars. The boat wobbled side to side.

"Get off! Are you crazy?" Danny looked fierce.

Adam looked at me like I had lost my mind.

"Stop it." Emma slammed her hand on the seat. "Do you want us to sink?"

"We found what we were looking for...we should go back," I said. Danny looked at me in disgust and Adam and Emma seemed to agree with him.

"Look." Emma pointed to the poachers' boat. It moved into the fiery ball, stopped, turned, and circled the ship's perimeter. It moved in and out of the fog until it disappeared behind the glow.

"They're nuts," Adam said.

"I'm not saying we go that close," Emma said. "A tiny bit more won't hurt."

"Stupid poachers, they don't know what they're doing," I said. "This is good enough." The strange stillness of the ship puzzled me. Around us the sea heaved, but the ship sat in calm waters. If there was anyone on board, they gave no sign. The sagging ropes and lack of sails gave it a ghostly appearance. The ship of death.

"They're not chicken, like some people," Danny said.

"Shut up. Just shut up!" I grabbed both oars.

"Let *go!*" Danny's elbow jabbed me below the ribs. I bent over, gasping for air. Straightening, I hurled myself at Danny and knocked both of us against the side of our boat. The sudden shift of weight tilted it to one side and water rolled in.

Emma gasped. I turned around and stared in astonishment as Adam sailed through the air. He dropped like a cannonball, disappeared beneath the surface, then bobbed like a cork to the top. For a moment he rode the crest of a wave, then he dropped down to the other side. The current tugged at him. The distance between us terrified me.

"Do something!" Emma screamed.

"Get the light on him." Frantically I felt for the rope.

"We're coming," Danny shouted.

"Hurry...hold the light steady." The rope shook in my hands.

Slowly, Danny narrowed the distance between Adam and our boat. Only then did I notice how dark it was. The light of the phantom ship had faded and plunged us into blackness. The ship had slipped back to its watery grave.

Chapter 25

❧

The flashlight swung back and forth.

"Sorry." Emma adjusted the light. "Oh god, I can't believe this."

"It's okay...I can reach him." I tugged on the rope, then held it above my head and tested its weight by swinging it around like a cowboy in a rodeo. It flew at Adam. The wind caught it, the rope dropped, and the waves dragged it several metres away. Adam raised one arm half out of the water before a wave slapped him in the head.

No one said anything. *Please, please let Adam get this rope.* I couldn't go home without him. A thousand-ton weight sat in my gut. I clenched my teeth, pulled the rope back in, and forced myself to concentrate. Emma held the light. Danny's breath came in short gasps. The rope flew through the air and landed half a metre from Adam.

"Grab it!" I screamed.

"Go!" Emma shined the beam of light on the rope. "You can do it!"

Adam tried to move against the waves. The life jacket bobbed him about, making him fight for every inch, but without it—well, I didn't want to think about that.

"He's got it—yes," Emma said. "Yes!"

"Way to go." Danny steadied the oars.

I braced my feet against the insides of the boat and with both hands began to haul the rope in. My palms burned, and I squeezed the rope until the veins on my arms popped. Adam looked like an orange buoy dragging through the water. Not much futher now. His hand reached for the side of the boat, the other clung to the rope.

"Hang on, I'll pull you up." I blinked water from my eyes.

Adam hung half in the water, his body resting against the hull, his eyes wide, fixed on the boat. His fingers squeezed the rope. The waves slapped the hull. Everyone held their breath.

Emma put the light down and together we tugged. Danny shifted his weight to the other side of the boat. Slowly, like an anchor, Adam inched up. He teetered on the gunnel, his legs kicking, then fell inside and rolled onto the bottom of the dory. Emma and I fell backward, landing in the water on the bottom of the boat. It rocked back and forth. I crawled up onto the seat in the stern and sat opposite Danny. The flashlight moved with the seat and threw weird shadows around the boat.

"Adam...sorry...I...." I felt like I might throw up. I closed my eyes for a minute.

"Oh my god, I thought we'd never get you out," Emma said. "Are you okay?" I opened my eyes and saw the flinch in Adam's face when Emma pulled on his arm.

"I want to go home."

"Yeah, well, I've had enough." Danny held the oars. "Anyways, the ship's gone."

Adam crawled up beside me, and like a small pup he pushed into my side. He shook so hard our seat vibrated. Some flesh had been scraped off his arm and blood dribbled onto the seat. His hair was plastered to his head and water was running down his face.

"Here." Danny handed his sweatshirt to Adam.

"Okay, that was totally weird," Emma said.

"And the strange light...just faded to nothing." My arms had goosebumps.

"Ghosts," Danny said.

"Hey, my camera." Adam's camera floated in the bottom of the boat. "It's waterproof."

"Good thing." I put it in my pocket.

The fog rolled over the white-topped waves. The sea had turned to what Dad called "a good chop." I looked around to get my bearings.

"Where's the compass?" I asked.

"Down there." Adam's finger shook as he pointed into the sea.

"We'll manage." I strained to see the shoreline against the dark grey of the sky.

"We could follow the stars, if we could see them," Adam said.

"I think it's that way." Emma pointed into the fog bank. She didn't give me a lot of hope, but we couldn't just sit here.

"I can take over," I said to Danny.

"Look," Adam pointed to starboard. "A light."

We watched it fade back into the fog, reappear, dip up and down, then vanish.

The sea heaved our boat up and down. Stars appeared between the clouds. I wished for the sounds of the harbour: the wail of the foghorn or the clang of a buoy—anything to suggest we were near land. The mysterious light on the water continued to follow us. It vanished for minutes then reappeared, the gap between us unchanged. We sat in tired silence. The sun would be up in three hours. Mentally, I made a list: our boat was sturdy, we had life jackets, water, granola bars, and a flashlight. Making it until morning shouldn't be a problem.

I pulled back on the oars. My chest filled with air and I blew it out slowly. We had seen the phantom ship and even had pictures to prove it. But I would be grounded for life.

"There," Emma said. "Did you hear it?"

"This is freaky," Danny whispered.

The muffled sound of an engine came through the fog.

"We've got to turn. We're heading right for the poachers," I pointed out.

"But the light's the other way," Adam whined.

"What do we do now?" Danny asked.

"Maybe it's our parents looking for us," Adam said hopefully.

"They're sleeping," Emma said. "Put out the light."

We sat in blackness. Adam was making puffing noises. I took a deep breath. The chugging of the engine grew louder. They had picked up speed.

"We can't outrun them," Danny said.

"Well I'm not just sitting here," said Emma.

She and I rowed faster, but Danny was right. Our boat wasn't going to outmaneuver a fishing vessel. Stabs of pain

DEBORAH TOOGOOD

travelled down my back. Exhausted muscles contracted and paralyzed my arms.

"Why are they after us?" Adam asked.

"'Cause they think we're following them," I answered. "We could have them thrown in jail."

"Oh no," Emma breathed. A beam of light swept across the water.

"These guys mean business," Danny said.

"Duck." I crouched down in the small dory.

Shouts. Again the light swept by. We were just a speck in the ocean. Why did we have to stumble across poachers? A minute passed. The light brushed the stern of the boat. I wondered if I could have a heart attack. I was ready to exhale when the beam of light fell on my back. Like a deer in headlights I froze. The men roared.

Chapter 26

❦

We cowered in the bottom of the boat. I had to look. I grabbed the edge and stuck my head up so that my eyes peeked over the side. The fishing boat had an open back deck to stack traps. Lobster traps hung at crazy angles. A small cabin sat forward. A man stood at the helm. Two guys leaned over the side, one holding the light on us.

"What are you doing?" Danny motioned for me to get down.

"There's three of them." I ducked my head.

"It's them kids." The voice sounded young.

"We'll fix them." If it was possible to know our fate by that guy's voice, then we were done.

The skipper gunned the engine.

"Holy god, they're going to ram us," Danny said.

"What'll we do?" Adam cried.

"Stay down," I said. "They're just trying to scare us."

"You'd better be right." Emma crouched down and put her arms over her head: crash position.

The roar of the engine pierced the air. Diesel fumes plugged my nose. I squeezed my eyes shut and prayed. *Please... help us.* The boat beat by. Its wake made us rock like crazy.

"Hang on," Danny shouted.

Waves sloshed over the side.

"We've got to bail," Emma said.

"I got it." Danny lunged for the bailer and began to madly throw water over the side.

"Hurry." Emma made a cup with her hands and scooped. Adam and I did the same. Walter kept rolling into our boat.

The *chug chug* of their engine slowed.

"What are they doing?" Adam grabbed my arm.

Their engines reversed. Water churned white. My heart began to hammer all over again.

"They're coming back," I said. We were easier prey than the lobsters crawling on the bottom of the ocean.

"Danny, fasten your life jacket." Emma checked Adam's straps.

Our boat was sitting low in the water. It hadn't occurred to me that we could sink—waiting the three hours until dawn had seemed like the worst thing that could happen.

The light continued to reach back and forth over the water. Then it found us. Emma grasped the oars. She tried to move us out of the spotlight.

"Ugh, it's no use," she said.

"Here they come." I braced myself.

"I'd like a chance to punch their lights out," Danny stuck his flashlight in the pocket of his cargo shorts and crouched down on his knees.

"Matt," Adam cried.

They were heading straight toward us. The white hull bore down. I saw the blur of the waterline stained with green barnacles and faded black numbers, stencilled near the deck. The hull may as well have been that of an ocean liner for all the chance we stood. It just kept coming. Adam's fingers bit into my arm. I held my breath.

"Oh my god...get ready to jump," Emma said.

"Stay with the boat," Danny said.

The boat passed by within a metre. A white blur.

"They're trying to swamp us," I shouted. These guys knew how it would look. An empty boat and four kids drowned. Our fault.

Miraculously, the four of us were still kneeling in our boat. But it wasn't over yet. Like a wild circus ride, the waves pitched us back and forth. Then the wake from their boat slammed over the side, and suddenly our boat was an over-flowing bathtub. We scrambled onto the seats. From a distance, their boat's engine idled. I prayed the poachers would keep going. The seat beneath me slowly dropped, my knees disappeared, and the water crept up to my chest. My bones were shaking out of control. Another minute and my body no longer sat on the seat; the life jackets we wore held us above the sinking boat. I gasped when the water circled my neck.

"Stay together." Emma signalled us to grasp hands.

"Help!" Adam began to drift with a wave.

"I've got you." I lunged for the loop at the back of his life jacket. My other hand clung to an oar. "Hang on!" I shouted.

Danny grabbed my oar with both hands and rested his chest on it.

"Everyone hold on," Danny said.

Emma wedged in beside Danny. I flipped Adam onto his belly. He squeezed his eyes and mouth shut. He'd had enough salt water. We all had. Like some kind of weird swimming drill, we huddled together, attached to the oar, and kicked.

Chapter 27

❦

We rode the top of a wave. Down and up again.

"Keep talking," Emma said.

"And don't close your eyes," added Danny.

We were clinging to an oar in the middle of the ocean because I'd wanted to show everyone I'd found the phantom ship. I couldn't imagine things would get worse.

"How much longer?" Adam asked.

"It's almost dawn; any minute we'll hear the boats," I said.

Danny looked at his watch and said nothing.

"Keep moving," I said. Danny, Emma, and I thrashed our legs in the water. Adam just hung on. The cold washed through my body, my fingers numb over the oar. I reminded myself it was August.

"I hear them, I hear them," Adam said. "The fishing boats are coming."

The drone of a single boat drifted over the water. The engine would speed up and then slow, searching. It grew louder.

"Help! Help!" Emma shouted.

"Over here," Danny screamed.

The boat chugged out of the mist, its single beam of light sweeping the sea. It slowed, a wooden boat with a small cabin up front. It had the same low-slung stern all fishing boats had along the Northumberland shore.

"No," Danny said.

The boat crept close enough for us to see the poachers.

"It can't be," I said. Two men stood alongside. "Why would they come back?"

"What'll we do?" Emma asked.

Adam began to cry.

I didn't care why they came back; we needed help. So what if they were poachers? We had to get out of the water. If I'd had a white flag, I would've waved it; instead I raised one arm. I surrendered. Let them think they won. I'd work on a plan.

"We have to get on that boat," I said.

"Are you nuts?" Danny asked.

"They sank my boat," Emma said. "Why would they help us?"

The two men leaned over the side. One held a long pole above his head and the other kept the light on us. I could see a third man in the cabin.

"Looky here, it's them kids, all right." The man with the pole looked like a bear. "Peter, get ready to catch us some fish."

Peter leaned over the side. "They're just kids," he said.

"Kids! Just trouble. Far's I'm concerned, not our problem," Pole Man said.

"It'll be your problem if you don't get yer arse in gear," the captain yelled from the cabin.

"Don't know how you convinced the old man to turn around," Pole Man grumbled to Peter.

"I'm not g-going to jail," Peter stuttered. "'Sides, they might know something."

DEBORAH TOOGOOD

"Knowing too much is the *problem*," Pole Man said.

"They might know about...about that ship," Peter said.

Pole Man looked at Peter. "Dunno...hey, Cap, what'll we do with 'em?"

"That idiot wanted to come back...put them in the back by the traps," Cap said. "There's plenty of rope."

"C-c-can't leave 'em out here," Peter said.

"Fish bait." Pole Man jabbed the water. "Yep, might have some fish bait."

Because of these boneheads, Emma's boat was on the bottom of the ocean. But whatever their reasons, they'd come back.

"Hey kid, grab this." Pole Man thrust a two-metre-long pole at us. The kind that once had a hook on the end.

"Danny, you go first," Emma said.

"I–I'll go," I stammered.

But Danny let go of the oar and kicked the few metres to the pole. Treading water, he reached out, arms straining, chin up, trying not to swallow the salt water; Pole Man yanked it back.

"Ha, missed." Pole Man grinned.

Danny reached again. Peter stepped in and put his hands on the pole. The two men hauled Danny up and swung the pole around until he hung over the boat. I heard the thud as he landed.

"I don't like that man," Adam said.

"Come on." I grabbed onto the back of his life jacket and dragged him to the hovering pole. "Just hang on." Adam's eyes widened, then he clenched his teeth and grabbed for the pole.

"Here's the runt." Pole Man flipped him up and over like a pancake.

The pole swung back.

"We don't got all night." Cap revved the engine.

Emma released the oar and reached up. Slowly she lifted out of the sea, her eyes on me, lips set in a straight line. Determined. She dropped to the bottom of the boat. The fishing boat began to creep forward, the pole trailing over the water. I let go of the oar and grabbed for the pole. Pole Man pushed the pole out farther. They were leaving me. I lunged at it, and my body lifted out of the water. The smooth wood pressed in my palms. I squeezed my fingers around the pole, and the boat dragged my legs through the water.

"Maybe you want to stay behind." Pole Man dangled me like a fish on a hook.

"C-come on, Mac, they—they might know about the ship." Peter inched the pole in until he could swing it around. I fell into the boat and flopped over onto my back. Pole Man—Mac—leered over me. His eyes were evil. He stood at least six feet tall and half as wide. I lay on the floor and watched him scratch his whiskers, the snake tattoo on his arm slithering up and down his bicep.

Chapter 28

❦

"**T**ie them up good." Mac shoved his boot into my thigh.

I wished I had a baseball bat or his pole in my hand, anything to smash that smirk off his face. But I swallowed the saliva in my mouth and lay there like some pathetic creature.

Peter moved like a robot. His arms jerked and his legs twitched and then he leaned in close and his nasty fish smell made me want to puke. He could've been the same age as Danny's brother, but lucky for me, he couldn't tie knots like Mitch.

"Jeez, do it right." Mac grabbed the rope then twisted Danny's arm behind his back.

"Just drop us near shore and we didn't see anything," Danny said.

"Think I'm stupid? I would've left you there," Mac said. "Still might." He turned and stumbled over a pile of rope. "Idiot." He shoved Peter against the traps, leaned down, grabbed the cross dangling from a chain around Peter's neck, and ripped it off. "Think that'll help you?" He threw it sideways. It sailed over the railing, caught the moonlight like a spark, and was gone in an instant.

Peter sprawled on the traps. He rubbed his neck, his mouth moved frantically. Hatred flickered on his face. He slowly got up, mumbled to himself, and shuffled into the cabin.

"Move it," Cap yelled. "Got cargo to unload."

The containers and traps lay haphazardly about the deck. The lobsters snapped at each other. These guys were total amateurs. They hadn't even bothered to band the claws.

Emma and Adam sat side by side, rope coiled around their legs, their hands behind their backs. Adam was bug-eyed. I wondered if he was in shock. Emma had that deep frown between her eyes. I'd seen that look when she'd lost a race.

Peter came back out. "Over here." He nodded to Danny's shackled body.

I wormed my way over. The wooden deck picked at my shorts. Peter finished tying my hands. Little hairs stood on my scalp. I'd take another shot at Peter.

"I wouldn't trust these guys," I said.

"Better keep quiet." Peter fumbled with my rope.

I looked at the others. A gob of snot ran down Adam's face and mixed with his tears. From the back of the boat we were lined up perfectly, like four sacrifices. I had a perfect view of their operation. They weren't fishers. Ropes lay in a tangled mess and tools were scattered across the deck. They'd stolen this boat. Maybe they'd abandon it.

"Watch them," Mac shouted from the cabin.

Peter sat on a trap, hugging himself, his eyes on the floor.

"I–I want to go home," Adam whimpered.

"They'll drop us off soon." I worked the rope twisted around my wrists.

Peter rubbed a spot on the floor with the heel of his rubber boot. "Not up to me."

"Kidnapping can get you fifty years," I said.

"Yeah, well I don't like this either. W-what you doing out here, anyway?" He balanced a toothpick on his lower lip, chomping down on it when he remembered it was there. "You chasing that fire ship?"

"The phantom ship," I said.

"Get too close and you'll burn," said Danny.

"It's full of pirates' ghosts," added Emma. "It's a death ship."

Peter's boot paused. The toothpick stopped moving. His eye twitched. "How you know about that?"

"We read about it," Adam said. "And a ghost rowed us in his boat."

"It's true, he saved us," I said.

"Peter! Get these lobsters in the bin," Mac shouted.

"Better keep quiet, don't wanna piss him off." Peter scrambled to his feet.

We lay on the floor. Stars dotted the sky. The sea had stopped heaving. Dawn must be close.

Chapter 29

A jab in my ribs.

"What?" I mumbled. Danny had rolled into me.

"Shh, you're jabbering away," Emma hissed. "About the ship...and death."

I shook my head to clear my brain. I must have dozed off.

"It's a ship of death, all right—our death," Danny said, glaring at me. "You've had some stupid ideas—"

"What do you mean?"

"Dragged us out here."

"I didn't twist your arm."

"Too scared to go out yourself."

"You wanted to find it too!"

"Phantom ship, phantom ship, that's all you talk about," Danny mocked. "Because of you we're stuck with a bunch of crooks."

"Danny." Emma rolled her body toward him. She managed to land a feeble kick on his legs.

"Don't fight," Adam said.

"You found your pirates," Danny shouted.

Mac stepped out of the cabin. "Shut up or I'll shut you up." He spat on the floor and went back inside.

"You're no better, Danny. *You're* the thief." I sucked in a lungful of air.

Danny's cheeks puffed out, his face darkened, and under the ropes his muscles strained. "What—"

"Matt, what are you saying?" Emma asked, confused.

"He stole money...from the team."

"What the hell are you talking about?" Danny said. "You've lost it."

"I saw you, after practice." My anger shocked me. Not making the team had hurt. Going to school the next day, I may as well have *cut* stamped across my forehead. Trying to be a good sport, I'd sat in Dad's car while the team washed it to make that money. "You took it from the equipment shed." I jerked my arms—the ropes loosened.

"You're nuts."

"The other day, I saw you at the field."

"And I gave it to Coach." Danny slammed both feet down on the boat bottom. "I'd never—"

"I said shut up." Mac fired a half-empty pop can at us. It caught Adam in the leg, then rolled across the deck, leaving a trail of foam.

No one said anything. The day at the soccer field replayed in my head. Danny in the shed, shoving the money in his pocket, running across the field. Talking to Coach. On the other side of the field. With his back to me. My gut sank.

"But—but I saw you put it in your pocket." Even as the words spilled out, I knew I didn't have all the facts.

"I can't believe it. How could you think that?" Danny asked.

"Danny wouldn't steal," Emma said.

She was right. Danny was my best friend. He wouldn't even keep a dollar he found on the locker room floor once. He took it to the office. My face burned. I twisted my body.

My hands clenched, and I pushed against the ropes. I felt my own sticky blood. My head was spinning. I had to get out of here. Emma and Danny were staring at me like I was some kind of lunatic. Adam kept his eyes on his feet.

"You're sick," Danny said.

"It's a mistake," Emma said. "Matt didn't mean it. Remember the time he thought I ate his lunch?"

Oh man, not just a mistake—a colossal screw-up. "Sorry. I'm sorry." I reached up to rub the tears off my face. Matt, Emma, and Adam stared at my free hand.

I wormed myself backward until my bum pressed against the stern. I felt Danny's flashlight dig into my behind. With both hands behind my back, I worked the ropes. The other hand slipped out. I tugged at the rope wrapped around my legs. I worked fast. My breath came in gulps. If I could free Danny, we might have a chance.

"Careful," Danny whispered. "Here he comes."

I stiffened like a corpse. The tangle of rope lay on my legs.

"We're done here." Peter reached for one of the traps. He lifted one end and dragged it to the front deck.

I had to act quickly. I groped for the flashlight behind me. *Got it.*

Adam met my eyes. "SOS," he mouthed.

With my back against the stern, I inched myself up until I stood even with the gunnel. My hands shook. I held my breath and whipped around to face the sea. The flashlight rested on the gunnel. I turned on the beam, three short dots, three long dots, three short dots, three long dots, three short, three long. *Please, please someone see this.* Three—

"No you don't!" Mac lunged.

His fist covered the top half of my head, and my feet dangled above the deck. I imagined my scalp separating from the rest of me. I got a whiff of his sweaty pits. He could gut me like a fish. Then his fist slammed into my belly.

I stopped breathing. I watched the flashlight roll across the deck. My legs wobbled. Danny, Emma, and Adam sat helpless, horror all over their faces. I dropped to the deck.

It started in my gut, the fire. Then I found my legs. Every muscle in my body tightened.

I charged at Mac. I pulled up like a bull, then hit low. My arms stretched around his bulk, my fingers going only as far as his armpits, and I clung onto him. His breath heated my face. With one hand I landed a punch to the side of his fat nose. Mac howled. He ripped me off his body so violently that I held bits of his shirt in my hands. He squeezed my diaphragm between his gigantic hands and raised me, like a prize, above his head. I heard the gasp of my shipmates.

Mac lunged again, his roar shaking my entire body, and then he launched me like a missile.

I sank.

Cold salt water filled my mouth, my nose, my ears. Hundreds of bubbles shot by me. But my life jacket didn't let me go. I bobbed to the surface. I gagged and spat and sucked at the air.

Far away there were screams, then the hard throttle of a boat's engine, and diesel filled the air. I watched the stern of the boat disappear.

I closed my eyes and cried.

Chapter 30

❧

I don't know how long I floated. I couldn't feel anything. Maybe I had hypothermia. My heart no longer hammered. I didn't want to kick. My life jacket rolled me over onto my back, and my head rested on the collar like a pillow. The stars twinkled. I wondered about heaven. It might be nice to sleep in the clouds. I closed my eyes and let the current carry me.

Stop it, I told myself. *Don't give up.* But I'd lived here all my life. How many times had I heard the phrase "lost at sea"? *But Danny's grandfather came back, full of tales. And we saw the phantom ship.*

A light moved over the water. A falling star. I couldn't take my eyes off of it. It came closer, closer still. Water slapped the hull of a boat. I tried to call. All I could manage was a pitiful croak. My eyes burned. Salt crusted on my eyelashes. I blinked once, twice, the light hitting my face.

"Help," I managed to squeak.

Soft sounds of water: a small boat. An old dory approached, the light at the stern. I tried to rub the salt from my eyes. A man rowed, his clothes loose, grey hair blowing in the wind. He couldn't be real. Like a dream I'd had before. Then I wanted to cry. It was him! The old man: the salty sailor. He had come for me.

My guardian angel steadied the boat. I held onto the side. I hooked one leg over, but gravity pulled me back into the water. With a grunt I lunged for the boat, I hollered, and all sixty-five pounds of me tumbled into the bottom. I crawled onto the seat in the stern and faced the sailor. A splinter stuck in my finger. I sucked on it and tasted the blood. I was alive. I filled my lungs. I was alive and in an ancient boat with a man I thought was a ghost.

He waited. Silent. He would take me home, to the beach. My parents would be waiting, but so would Aunt Molly, and Danny and Emma's families. What could I do? Mac would finish me off if I tried to follow now. It didn't matter that I did ten push-ups every night before bed, or that I could run faster than anyone in my grade.

I gripped the seat with both hands. "My friends. We have to find that fishing boat." There was no time to go for help. "These guys are in a hurry."

His eyes flickered.

⁓

The light threw a spooky shadow over his face. His shirt flapped around his body like it covered a skeleton. With each push of the oars, the sailor would lean forward, then straighten his elbows and pull all the way back. Over and over again, like a machine. The strange part was I started to feel better. I was breathing normally, and as far as I could tell my heart had stopped banging in my chest. I sat up straight and lifted my head. Like a superhero, I'd battle the bad guys.

The sailor didn't speak and I wondered if he was breathing. But he knew where he was going. In one expert move, he whipped the dory around and followed a path through the sea.

"We sent an SOS," I said. I knew by now he wasn't a talker. "The poachers have my friends." The scar on his face didn't move.

I was more curious than afraid. My stomach did that little flutter and my detective senses tingled. Who rows around at night? And why had he taken us to Mrs. Hatfield's beach that first time? Could he be her grandfather who'd been lost at sea? I'd figure that out later. Whoever he was, he was a friend.

The sound of the oars, the up and down of the sea, reminded me that we were moving closer to my fate. I didn't have a plan.

Chapter 31

❦

The sky brightened. I turned to my right and saw the fiery orange ball. It moved closer, bigger, until the light fell on our dory. *Holy cow.* I could see the ship. Again. The light grew bigger and bigger. It was massive. The sea lit up like we were in a giant football stadium.

"It's the phantom ship—look," I said, turning to the sailor. He just kept pulling on the oars, and when I turned back to look at the ship, another boat was visible.

"It's them!" I pointed to the poachers' boat.

It had stalled; the waves were pushing its starboard side dangerously close to the phantom ship. In the light, I saw the three poachers standing at the tip of the bow. They were leaning so far I thought they would fall overboard.

"What the heck?" I heard Cap say.

"It's what those kids said—get us closer," Mac yelled.

"We don't know what we be dealing with," Cap said. "We'll hold her steady."

The poachers were so busy gawking, I figured we could parade right in front of them.

My eyes pulled back to the phantom ship. The salty sailor had rowed our boat around to her far side. I sucked my breath in. The ship was awesome. From the curved timbers, three masts stretched up all the way to the clouds.

The crow's nest perched on the main mast, but there was no sign of a watch. No sails, no rat lines ran across the rigging, and no pirates. Danny's grandfather would say this ship was a beauty. The front was decorated with a woman carved of wood, her long hair flowing past the bow. A huge brass bell sat mid-deck. It was magnificent.

The sailor rowed us so close by the stern of the ship I could touch it. I didn't feel any heat on my skin, and thought maybe it was the effect of falling overboard, and everything that had happened to me, having numbed my senses. I was beyond thinking this was weird. I breathed in fresh salt air.

The sailor rowed past the phantom ship, around to the bow, and crept alongside the poachers' boat. The poachers stood with their backs to us. Peter had his hands in his pockets and Cap scratched his head. Mac looked twice as thick as I remembered.

"They're tied up in the back," I whispered. At least, I hoped so.

I stood up. I couldn't see them. I would have to board their boat. The old sailor pulled alongside. He pushed the oars down and held his boat still. His eyes met mine, and I realized this light show was my cover. He looked down to the floor of the dory. A knife, the type used to gut fish, lay in a leather sheath.

An electric charge took over my body. It started in my head, then moved down my limbs, and jolted me into action. With the knife between my teeth, I grabbed the buoy hanging over the edge of the poachers' boat and climbed onto the back deck. I turned to give the sailor the "okay" signal, but he had pushed off. His back was bent forward and his hands were locked on the oars. Then he was gone.

Chapter 32

❦

The orange light flooded the poachers' boat like a circus. I almost expected to see fireworks. The light boiled up out of the ocean, brighter and brighter. If anyone had been looking out to sea from shore, they would have thought they saw a UFO. But I was too exposed. If one of the poachers turned around, I'd be toast. *I can't waste time—soon the show will end.* My feet landed on the same deck I'd been pitched off of. Danny, Emma, and Adam lay together on the floor, their eyes glued to the phantom ship.

"Hey," I whispered.

Danny and I locked eyes. Emma and Adam stared at me like I was a ghost.

"Careful." Danny jerked his head toward the bow.

I ducked behind a lobster trap. Peter went into the cabin. He came back out, stopped, scratched his head, and looked right at us. He shrugged and went back to the front deck. We let our breath out.

The knife was sharp. The ropes fell off easily. Emma snuck into the cabin. She signalled Adam to follow her. I looked at Danny; we both knew Mac had to be taken out first.

I stuck the knife into the waistband of my shorts and waved Danny behind me. We crept along mid-deck, then tucked ourselves into the narrow passage alongside the cabin. From the window of the pilothouse, Emma gave a thumbs-up. Danny and I made it to the front of the cabin. Once we stepped out, we would be totally exposed. I stared at the massive back of Mac. My heart hammered.

"Follow 'em." Mac jabbed a thick finger toward the phantom ship.

"It's g-ghosts," stammered Peter.

"I'm staying here," said Cap.

"Might be treasure...look at her," argued Mac.

"You'll go without me," said Cap.

"Throw one of them kids on, we'll know if there's trouble," Mac suggested.

Cap spat on the floor and looked at Peter. He put his hands on his hips and glared at Mac.

"I'll not be doing time for your foolishness," Cap said. "We'll drop them at the point—gives us plenty of time to clear out of here."

"Yeah, we never sh-should have listened to you, Mac." Peter moved over closer to Cap.

"Maybe *you* wanna visit the ship of fire." Mac moved closer to Peter.

"Perfect." I mouthed to Danny. We had a straight run at him. I felt for the smooth wood of the knife's handle.

Danny pressed his hand on my back.

"Payback time," I growled. My voice sounded like someone else's.

I dropped the knife onto the deck and squeezed my hand into a fist. My heart pounded too fast. I took a deep breath and lunged at Mac. To my surprise, I landed a solid punch right on his nose.

"Stop it! Stop this on my ship!" Cap shouted.

Mac held both hands over his nose. He staggered backward, then his feet tangled in the rope lying on the deck. He lost his footing and fell back hard against the gunnel. The momentum pushed him up the side of the boat. His upper body dangled over the ocean, his legs waving madly. He teetered on the edge of the boat like a pendulum.

"Take this!" Peter rushed forward and threw Mac's legs in the air. The splash shocked us into action.

"Get Cap." I propelled myself forward.

"Peter, get—" Cap gave his last order.

I jumped on Cap's back. My arms stretched around his chest. Danny tackled him, and we crashed to the floor. We rolled around. I was on top and then I was under him and I heard Danny's punches land on his back. Cap floundered like a fat fish.

"The rope, get the rope!" Emma shouted.

Danny and I wrestled him down until we both sat on his chest. Even Adam got in a few decent punches. Peter grabbed the rope. We tied Cap's arms and legs. Then he just sagged.

"You kids are crazy, you can't run this boat," Cap sputtered. "Peter, get these ropes off me."

We looked at Peter.

"D-don't th-throw me over, I c-can't swim." He put his arms up in the air.

"You can help us," Emma said.

I ran to the side of the boat and peered down at the water. "He's gone."

Either the ocean swells had carried Mac away, or he had just sunk to the bottom like a stone.

Chapter 33

✑◦◦

"The ship's g-gone." Peter looked bewildered.

He was right. To the east I could see the first streak of red on the horizon. Soon the sun would burst over the flat sea. I stared at where the phantom ship had been.

"We've got to report a man overboard," I said.

"Aw, leave him," Danny said. "He threw you in."

"We have to," I insisted.

The cabin windows wrapped around three sides and the back gapped open. A compass sat in the dash, just in front of the large wooden wheel.

"I want to steer," Adam said.

"You can help me." Emma had her hands on the wheel.

"Th-throttle's fussy, ease it up," Peter said.

The engine sputtered, then began a steady chug.

"Southwest it'll be," Emma decided.

"A radio." Adam picked up the microphone.

"It's a shortwave," I said.

Adam flicked a switch and turned the dial. A red light came on and static filled the cabin.

I grinned at him. He wiped his nose with the back of his toothpick arm.

"You try," Adam said.

"Testing...testing...." Static. "Matt Simmons here...we got a poacher."

"I don't think anyone's listening," Adam said.

I thought of Mac sinking in the water. "Man overboard—"

"Land!" Emma said. I saw the red banks of the Northumberland shore. A trail of tiny houses led to the harbour. Soon the fishing boats would chug out to sea.

Danny stepped into the doorway. "Man, did you see Matt?"

"He saved us," said Adam proudly.

"You were something else, shouting and jumping at Mac like that—a hero," Emma said.

"I wouldn't want to tangle with you." Danny punched me in the shoulder.

I blushed and tried not to smile too much. I stood in the cabin beside my friends and watched the channel markers slide by.

Chapter 34

❧

"**A**lmost home," Emma said.

"Now we have to park this thing," said Danny.

"Let Matt." Emma stepped away from the wheel.

I stood at the wheel, my hands spread wide. The wood felt solid and smooth. My chin came to the top of the wheel, my eyes barely over it.

Fishers dressed in yellow pants and dark rubber boots worked on their boats. They shouted to each other, stacked lobster traps, and prepared for their day. They stopped and stared when our boat chugged into the harbour.

I pulled back on the throttle and the engine slowed to a low growl.

"Over there." Emma pointed to what I hoped was a large opening. Several tires had been nailed to the side of the dock. The fishers on shore moved over to catch the rope Danny was ready to throw. Adam stood by me in the pilothouse.

I cut the engine and prayed the waves would guide us in. "Oops!" I grinned at Adam. Our boat hit the dock hard and bounced back and forth before settling in against the tires nailed to the pilings.

Just as we stepped out of the cabin, an RCMP cruiser pulled up and Officer McNab stepped out. He jumped the half-metre gap and landed on the deck of the boat.

"Well, thought I'd seen everything." He walked over to where Cap lay under several layers of rope. "Just called your parents, they're on their way," he said to me.

I looked at Adam and wondered what it would be like to be grounded for the rest of my life.

"Oh, and the coast guard received a call about poachers...seems they picked one up clinging to a buoy, crying like a baby."

I raised my hand and high-fived Danny. Emma and Adam joined in.

"Mac crying, I'd like to see that," I said.

"Yeah, *wah*, *wah*," Adam said.

"Who's this?" Office McNab looked at Peter.

Peter stepped forward.

"I...I didn't mean to hurt anyone, and I'm sorry I went along with Mac and Cap."

"Well, we'll take it from here; there'll be some paperwork, but I guess it can wait," Officer McNab said, and he escorted Peter to his car.

One of the fishers put down a gangplank and I led the way through the crowd. I'd be lying if I said I didn't like the slaps on my back.

Chapter 35

❦

I followed Dad out to the front lawn.

"Want some help?" I asked.

"About done here." Dad set his paintbrush in the empty tin. "Just need to check those beach stairs."

I trailed behind, my eyes on the back of his work shirt.

I stopped at the top of the cliff. The ocean stirred up a blue so deep it hurt my eyes. Whitecaps rode the top of the waves, and a ship bobbed on the horizon.

"Fall's not long off." Dad jumped on the first step. "She should hold for the winter." He sat down. I squeezed past him to the step below. For a while we just watched the sea.

Saying goodbye to Adam had been hard. We'd told our parents about the phantom ship and the old sailor who had saved our lives both times. They were hard to convince, and in the end, it was catching the poachers that saved my hide. But I was still grounded.

"Well, best be getting back for lunch," Dad said.

"Hey, whose truck?" I saw wild grey hair. "Mrs. Hatfield!"

She pulled over next to us. "Well, young man, back from another adventure on the high sea."

We looked at each other for a minute, then she reached inside to the seat of her truck and picked up a wiggling bundle.

"Sophie had her litter." A fat brown pup tried to climb up her sweater.

I looked at the pup. The blood pumped in my face and I felt prickly all over. I reached out my hands and the warm weight fell into my arms. A wet nose pushed into my neck. And then he settled down to clean my face. I giggled.

"Can we keep him?" I begged Dad.

Dad folded his arms against his chest, tilted his head sideways and studied the pup. But not for too long.

Dad sighed. "Well, I guess we have a new family member." He shook Mrs. Hatfield's hand.

"I'm going to call him Salty." I already knew he would be a sea dog. "Just a minute." I handed Salty to Dad.

My feet flew over the yard and up the stairs to my room. I yanked my sock drawer open and felt around until my fingers clutched smooth metal. I left the old coin in my drawer for luck, but took the tooth.

I ran back down and put it in Mrs. Hatfield's hand and closed the deal.

"What's this?" she asked.

"I found it in the dory that rowed us ashore," I said.

She looked at the tooth in the palm of her hand. "In the old days, they used gold to fill teeth," she said. "Maybe you should hang onto this."

"No, it's yours," I said. She gave me a strange look, nodded, and put it in her pocket.

"Tell you what, I'll put it away for safekeeping," Mrs. Hatfield said.

I carefully picked up Salty and held him against my chest and breathed in his puppy smell.

It would be a long time before I saw Mrs. Hatfield again. But on that day I wrote in my notebook *Mrs. Hatfield investigation closed.*

The cold ocean wind blew in my window. I still smarted from my grounding, but I lived in the best place in the world. Salty would grow and become my friend, and maybe someday we would have an adventure.

DEBORAH TOOGOOD

Epilogue

I smooth out the newspaper and read it again. *Heroes.* I cut around the picture. Upstairs, I go over to my bulletin board and push a thumbtack into each corner of the newsprint. Lying on my bed, I tuck my hands behind my head and look at the two pictures. In Aunt Maddy's photo, Adam, in his city clothes, stands next to me. I stare at the photo: Four friends. Matted hair, no shoes, wet shorts and T-shirts. Big grins. I look closer: I've gotten taller.

I slide off my bed. On my desk lies a pile of pictures. Fog on glossy paper. Adam's pictures. I pin one up between the two other photos, then step back and smile. Even if I strain my eyes I can't see it. Nothing. Not a bit of light or fire, and certainly no old sailor. Not even three towering masts.

After all, it's a ghost ship.

Acknowledgements

~⌒~

Many thanks to Marsha Skrypuch for her early encouragement of this project. Thanks also to Alexander MacLeod for his creative writing class, to Sheree Fitch for reading my manuscript, and to the editors at Nimbus Publishing for smoothing out the bumps along the way.